I0618953

THIS WORLD AND THE NEXT

SHELLY JARVIS

PAPER MAGE PUBLISHING

Copyright © 2022 by Shelly Jarvis

All rights reserved.

No part of this book may be reproduced in any form or by any electronic or mechanical means, including information storage and retrieval systems, without written permission from the author, except for the use of brief quotations in a book review.

CONTENTS

FIELDS OF QUAY

Originally published in *Deep Space* by Black Hare Press

CHAPTER 1

There are two facts universally accepted about Magic Doors: the first is that they never stay exactly where you put them, and the second is that, be they inside or out, they can only be seen after it rains.

Garret Finley was thinking on these facts, and Magic Doors in general, when, from the corner of his eye he was certain he spied the Duke of Islington walking past.

Duke Reginalt MacReoch XII of Islington, referred to as the Dark Duke in impolite society (which, of course, was a perfect descriptor of Finley), was unlikely to be in a place of ill repute such as this. He ruled an outlying planet, sure, but even the poorest of the system's planet-keepers were rich, though maybe not respected. Anything he could want was at his disposal, or could be purchased and brought to him at the press of the button on his credit-comm. Yet he was here, in the same hole-in-the-wall as Finley, rubbing shoulders with all the wrong folks.

Finley took a sip of his electric-blue helio-vodka. The menu called it a *Turpain Stunner*, but the only thing stunning about it was how violently drunk it made you after about three sips. Quick, effective, and most importantly, cheap.

Perhaps that was why he saw it in the hands of nearly everyone in the bar.

Finley turned toward where he'd spotted the Dark Duke, checking to see what he was drinking. Red, fizzy, with black bubbles clinging to the bottom. Not a poor man's drink. Something with cloves, anise, or some other useless herb imported from beyond Door Three. Finley wondered what the tonic was called, while hating his own curiosity.

He sneered. He hated the Dark Duke, too. For his stupid drink (why couldn't the bastard just order a get-drunk-quick item with the noxious liquor overpowered by a strong fruit like everyone else), his filthy rich-ness, and a petromic assload of other reasons. Why in the four hells of Hectron was the Duke in the Tuscorion Tavern in the first place? And, now that he thought about it, how had he *walked* past when Finley was absolutely certain the Duke of Islington had no legs?

Finley's thoughts were kindly interrupted when a dark-skinned man stumbled against the table, gripping the edge with his long fingers. He was tall, well-built, and had an air of mystery about him.

Finley smiled up at him, struck yet again by how handsome Oscar Temiteo was. Finley watched as Oscar sat down. He looked into his strange eyes—white, glowing orbs without a pupil. The lack of color was a defect from Oscar's techplant, but the tech itself was still functional and the weird eyes made him stand out and blend in simultaneously; most found it easy to forget everything else about him. Not Finley. He drank in each of Oscar's movements as he stored them into his mind with a million other small moments they'd shared.

Oscar pulled a stibby from his shirt pocket. He lit it, took a puff, and said, "Loo was full. Pissed in the alley."

"Oscar," Finley sighed, "didn't you learn from the incident on Purdri? These Regency fucks are obsessed with where you pull out your dick. Don't get yourself arrested on another shit planet."

"Can't promise. Shit planets are my bread and butter," Oscar said with a smirk. He tipped his head toward the Dark Duke and asked, "MacReoch in the corner?"

Finley nodded.

"Where'd he get the legs?"

"Dunno," Finley said, taking his second sip of the *Turpain Stunner*. With a shrug he said, "Maybe that's why he's on-world."

Oscar took another drag, exhaled slowly, and narrowed his eyes at the Duke. "Nah. Coulda got 'em closer to home and had 'em covered in gems or some such shit. Or wired up into his nervous system as to be useful. But them's not special-made. Don't even look like they fit him proper. More like trash metal if I'm bein' truthy."

Finley nodded. "Maybe he's on a rendezvous."

Oscar said, "Doubtful. Both his husband and wife are beauteous things. Why would he downgrade to that lot?"

Finley studied the people at the Duke's table. There were no great beauties among them, sure, but perhaps they were overflowing with personality. Finley was about to remark as much when a waitress leaned over their table.

"What can I get you?"

Finley pointed to his drink. "Probably nothing. I'm already at two sips."

"Lightweight, eh?" She smirked and asked, "If you change your mind, the Charpot '112E is particularly flavorful."

Finley took a hard look at the waitress. She had thick blonde hair pulled into a ponytail. She was tall and slender, but definitely hiding a bit of muscle under the uniform. She certainly wasn't like the usual townie messenger, but there was no mistake about it: she had given the code word.

Now the transaction began. Every word between them meant something else, a thousand other things, and his life might depend on whether or not he could decipher them. He scrubbed a hand through his curly brown hair, hoping to the high hells this woman wasn't as bad as the last one had been.

"Charpot is acceptable," he replied, confirming his under-standing.

"Lightyear for me," Oscar added. "Twist o' lime."

The girl nodded and walked back to the counter. Finley turned back to his partner. Oscar was running diagnostics behind his eyes. Most people wouldn't notice, but Finley could see the change. The corner of Oscar's eyes took on a slight blue hue, blended so well into the white that it was nearly invisible.

"Whaddya got?" he asked, running his finger over the rim of his glass. He wanted to take a swig, but knew he'd be wasted with that third sip.

"Two of his companions have records," Oscar said. "The one with the ponytail and the man with the serpent on his thigh." Finley began to turn toward their table, but Oscar grabbed his hand and whispered, "Don't look. The woman with the shaved head is surveying the room. She might have ears."

Finley put his hand over Oscar's and laughed. "Oh, honey, that's hilarious."

The waitress reappeared with their drinks. "Here you go, boys."

"Thanks," Finley said.

"Shit, shit, shit," Oscar mumbled

"You wanna pay up now or keep a credit open?" she asked, as if nothing was out of the ordinary.

"We'll pay now," Finley said. He leaned his arm toward the waitress and pulled up his sleeve so she could access his credit-comm. She hovered over him for a moment and Finley used her as a shield to ask, "What's wrong?"

The waitress cut in, saying, "Four hundred and eighty-seven credits, and a nice tip if you wanna be a sweetheart. Some gib over there only left me a thirty-seven credit. Can you believe that? After working a double shift like this, almost makes me regret my career choice."

Finley and Oscar looked at each other, both acutely aware of the waitress' number choice. Their ship was docked at 37.2, and apparently there was a problem. Finley saw Oscar's eyes tinge blue again. He turned to the waitress and said, "Double shift, eh? What time you get off?"

"Whenever I want."

She purred in a way that made Finley think of sex. He felt heat creep up his collar. This girl was damn good at playing her part. Too good for a shithole post like this. Townies were just supposed to relay intel, and they were guaranteed to screw it up one way or another, but she seemed to know exactly what to say and how to say it.

She leaned over the table and her breasts practically fell out of her top. Finley turned away so fast his neck cracked. But the woman didn't seem to notice his embarrassment. Or she didn't care. Finley turned tentatively back toward her. She hadn't moved an inch. She was either wildly confident or the gesture was completely non-sexual. *Probably both,* Finley thought. *I'm shit at reading people.*

The woman smirked, finally acknowledging the discomfort in Finley's disposition. She said, "Supposed to be off at four, if you're interested in hanging around. But if I have to stay over it may be closer to five."

Finley glanced past her to the Duke's table. Another man with a violent scowl had joined them, taking their party from four to five. She was good all right.

Oscar's eyes cleared and he seemed to just now realize the waitress was still here. She gave him a nod and asked, "Anything else for you?"

"One last thing," Oscar said, emptying his Lightyear in one gulp. "We're looking for some odd jobs while we're around this system. Any idea where we could pick some up?"

"Not right off," she said, pretending to think. "Maybe Old

Ethel could help you out. He's up on Mrathi in sector-4, right on the main drag, big gold sign out front."

"Thanks," Oscar said.

The girl walked away, checking on some other customers and collecting empty glasses as she went. As Finley watched her walk away, he asked, "How do you wanna play it?"

"Easy," Oscar said. "But the girl with the ears is Regency, so it's probably gonna get rough."

"Hold steady," Finley replied. "The waitress is delivering their drinks. Maybe she'll give us a distraction."

Finley watched the woman glide toward the table, a tray balanced on one arm. She sat the drinks down and talked to the newest arrival.

"Wait, that's not her," Finley whispered.

"How can you tell? All these blondes look the same."

Finley shrugged, his eyes roaming the tavern. "So where is our girl?"

Before the words were out of his mouth, one of the Duke's companions erupted into a coughing fit and fell against the table gasping for air. Taking their cue, Finley and Oscar jumped from their table and made a mad dash for the door. Finley turned as he reached it to see the others shove the waitress aside, pull their weapons, and head after them.

Finley followed Oscar through the narrow streets, their feet banging against the rickety planks of the boardwalk. He heard the Duke's people behind them, shoving townies out of their way. Once or twice he heard a splash as someone was pushed into the murky water beside the floating town. Oscar must've heard the splashes as well, because he ducked between two domed buildings into an alley that led away from the main drag. Finley hoped they could avoid getting a bunch of townies stuck in the middle of a firefight. Again.

Oscar was attempting to direct them to their ship, but in his effort to keep away from innocent bystanders, he'd inadvertently led them into a dead end. They turned around as soon as they realized their mistake, only to find themselves facing the business end of three blasters.

The Duke was nowhere in sight.

"Put your weapons down and keep your hands where I can see 'em," the woman with the shaved head said.

Finley and Oscar did as they were told.

Clearly the leader of the group, she sent one of the others to grab the weapons from the ground. She had an air about her, as if she was used to having flunkies do her bidding, and she seemed to enjoy her limited power. She wore a tight fitting leather jumper that bulged over her muscular arms and robust belly. The jumper was old (older than her, if she was natch and not a freezer-rebirth) and impractical for the smothering humidity of Nim-6.

"Well, well," she said, her oily voice causing an immediate squirming reaction from Finley. "Didn't expect to find a couple of Door Riders all the way out here. Thought it was a joke when the orders came through."

"Whose orders were they, anyway?" Finley asked.

Old suit laughed, her flunkies joining in. She smirked and said, "Stun 'em and let's get off this miserable globe."

Before the stunners were out of their holsters, both of the goons fell forward onto the grimy alley. Old suit spun around to find a .103-pulser mere inches from her face.

"Hi there," the waitress said, as if she were there to take the woman's drink order. "One breath out of place and I'll pulse your brains out of your head."

Old suit seemed to gather her courage before she took a deep breath, then spit in the waitress' face. She reached for her blaster, but her hand didn't make it an inch before the waitress' finger twitched on the trigger.

The force of the pulse blew Finley and Oscar back against the alley walls. Flying through the air, Finley thought, *Huh. Her brains really did pulse right out the back of her head.*

The waitress wiped the spit from her face, then stepped

over old suit's body. She stood with her hands on her hips, staring at the men as they clambered to their feet.

"I told you 37.2 was no longer an option," she said. "Why did you come this way?"

"We forgot," Finley said.

She sighed. "Well, running for your lives will do that to you. Grab your guns and follow me."

She turned around and walked back out the way they had come, Finley and Oscar following wordlessly behind her. Finley noted the grace and ease with which the waitress seemed to take in her surroundings as she checked for danger. He furrowed his brows and asked, "You're a townie?"

She glanced over her shoulder. "Like none you've ever seen."

THE WOMAN LED THEM OUT OF THE CITY TO AN AIRSTRIP LONG deserted because of its insistence on sinking into the swamp.

"Blasters ready, boys," she whispered back as they made their way into the hangar.

They edged around the corner and behind some boxes. There was a small freighter-class ship in the hangar, a huge tarp trying to camouflage it from prying eyes. Around the ship Finley saw a dozen figures, all carrying huge weapons.

"We'll never be able to take them all," Oscar whispered.

"We don't need to," the waitress said, smiling.

She stepped around the boxes and waved to the closest man. The man aimed his gun at her chest and called another man to him. Finley watched as the waitress headed straight toward the men with guns pointed at her, astonished by her reckless bravado.

"Doc," she said as she reached the older of the two men. "Good to see you."

The man lowered his weapon and pulled her into a hug. "Good to see you, too. We weren't sure you'd make it."

"Wouldn't miss it," she said.

The other man had turned back to his post, leaving her with the grey-haired leader. She waved for Finley and Oscar to join her, which they reluctantly did.

"We've got everything prepped and ready for you, Quay," the man said. "The guy from the bar is already onboard, detained in your quarters."

"Right," Quay said. "Did you relieve him of his coughing?"

"Kimby gave him a dotal strip when he picked him up from the club, but he'll need another in four hours. His throat will be raw for a few days, but he'll be well enough for interrogation by tomorrow."

"Good. I want to know who he's working for before we hit the Door."

"Come on Quay, you already know."

"No," she said, "not for sure. These guys weren't there for me, Doc, they were there to catch these Riders."

"What about the Duke?" Finley piped up.

Doc put his hands on his hips and looked him over. Finley felt like a hanrius being appraised for slaughter. Finally Doc growled, "Let him go. Not much we could do with a planetkeeper. Regent would be on us in an instant."

Doc pointed to the ship and the camo netting was removed. The engines were purring softly, barely audible even at such close range. Doc and Quay headed toward the ramp, Finley and Oscar following behind.

"You boys ready to go?" she asked.

"Where?" Finley asked.

"Door Nine."

"Nine?" Finley asked. "There is no Door Nine. And we're looking for Six, anyway. That's the whole point of us being out here."

"You're not gonna find Six out here," Quay laughed.

"We heard a rumor—"

Quay cut him off and said. "Just get on the fucking ship."

"We have our own ship," Oscar said.

"Not anymore," Doc replied. "It blew up about an hour ago."

"Blew up?" Oscar asked, shock and fear fighting for control of his voice. Their ship was his pride and joy, and Finley had a feeling the idea of being without it had never entered his mind.

"The bounty hunters who were chasing you must've contacted the Regent, because there were troops around that ship within ten minutes of your dock and departure. They sent a full troop inside, probably looking for information on the Doors."

"Damn it," Finley said.

"Wait," Oscar said. "If the troops were inside looking for information, how did it get blown up?"

The old man looked a bit sheepish. "Well, we couldn't let them have what they were looking for, could we?"

"You blew up my ship? YOU BLEW UP MY SHIP!"

Finley grabbed Oscar as he reached for his blaster, but it was pointless. One of the other guards had already stunned him. Oscar slumped toward the floor, Finley barely catching him before his body hit the ground.

"Pick him up. We've gotta go," Quay said. "We've wasted enough time already."

Finley hoisted Oscar over his shoulder and climbed the ramp. Without a ship, they didn't have a choice. They could go with this psycho waitress and her crew or become townies like the rest of the stranded nobodies on Nim-6,

"There are bunks to the left," Quay said, nodding toward a cabin. "I'll need you up front when you're finished."

Finley put Oscar on a bunk and headed toward the cockpit. "Where's the rest of your crew?"

"Not coming with us. They've got business elsewhere. You know how to pilot?"

Finley smirked. "Enough."

"Good. You've got about thirty seconds until we're spaceborne."

He familiarized himself with the craft. The controls of most ships were straightforward once you'd flown a few, so Finley had no trouble adjusting to the new ship's layout.

"Prepare hyperdrive," Quay said. "I want to hit it as soon as we clear orbit."

"Right," Finley said. "Calculations?"

"Unnecessary," she replied. "They're completed and locked. Just be ready to hit the switch when I tell you."

Finley bit back his response. He was the one who normally gave commands, but after being rescued by this woman more than once today, he didn't feel like he should be arguing. Besides, he'd been looking for Door Six for two years without success. If this woman could take him to it, after he helped her not find her imaginary Door Nine, all the better for him.

CHAPTER 2

"We've got incoming," Quay said, breaking into Finley's thoughts. "Two Regency HFPs on our tail and it looks like there's a full IPT waiting just outside of orbit."

Finley looked at the monitor. "Nim-6 is closing their shield."

"Damn it. Regent must've told 'em to lock us in."

"You've got about fifteen seconds before it closes," he said.

"Hold on. It's going to be a tight squeeze."

Quay adjusted the yoke, pitching the ship to fit through the closing shield. She kicked the power up as high as she could. Finley's teeth rattled inside his head and he felt himself pushed against the seat. The noise of the craft was a cacophony around them; hums and rattles, beeps and screeches sang through the ship.

"Oh shit, oh shit, oh shit," he mumbled as he squeezed his eyes shut.

The silence was like a smack in the face. It engulfed them, the nothingness vibrating through the air. Finley opened one eye. They were through the shield. He opened the other eye and stared at the massive transfer ship hovering ahead of them. The laser cannons on the side shifted toward them.

He glanced at the radar and felt a slight relief. "The HFPs are locked in the shield."

"That IPT isn't," Quay replied as lasers sprayed their starboard side. She flipped a couple switches on the control board and said, "Hyper drive on my mark: three, two, one."

Finley punched the hyper drive and watched the pinpoints of stars become star lines, and the star lines become blackness. It was a familiar and comforting sight, especially after the trouble they'd somehow just escaped. Quay still stared at the monitors, checking for any sign of pursuit. After a moment, she sighed and switched the ship to autopilot.

"That was fun," she said, a genuine smile on her face.

"Most fun I've had all week," Finley replied.

She reached her hand toward him and said, "Perian Quay, Dunner's Mark."

"Garret Finley, Hofstarn. My parents are originally from Dunner's Mark though."

"No shit? Small galaxy. Related to Jack Finley, by chance?" she asked, brows furrowed.

"I am. You know him?"

"Oh yeah," she said, her lips curving up.

"Were you a student of his?" Finley asked.

A look of confusion crossed Quay's face for a moment before she said, "I guess you could say that, though I like to think I taught him a few things." She saw a grimace on Finley's face and cleared her throat, saying, "Everybody knows Jack. He's a force, ya know? You his kid brother or something?"

"Jack Finley is my dad."

Quay laughed. "Couldn't be. Jack's what, twenty-six or so?"

"We must be talking about different people," Finley said. "Dad is from Ebriton on DM."

"So is my Jack."

"He's fifty-six. Married to Esme Patur."

"Esme Patur?" Quay asked, her face coloring in anger. "That little bitch. I *knew* she was after Jack."

"Hey, whoa. I dunno what you're on about, but you can't talk about my mom like that."

Quay ground her teeth together and stared hard into Finley's eyes. "Are you fucking with me? About Jack and Esme?"

"No, I'm truthy hundred," Finley replied. "But I don't know why you're upset about a wedding that happened twenty-eight years ago."

Quay turned and looked out into the blackness of space, staring at nothing for several moments. When she turned back to Finley, her face was deadly serious.

"I need you to tie me up."

"Excuse me?"

"Look at me, Finley. How old am I?"

"Uh, I don't know, mid-twenties?"

"Twenty-five," she said, her voice controlled, "or at least I was, when I took this gig. But you just told me that someone who I was in Flight School with, someone who I trained beside, someone I was engaged to, has been married for twenty-eight years."

Finley stared into her olive eyes and saw the turmoil within, and fear began to grip him as well. "You've been gone twenty-eight years?"

"I've been gone for nine months, Finley. At least, that's all I remember."

"This is crazy. It's impossible."

"Maybe," she said. "Maybe not."

"How?"

"I don't know. There are a lot of scenarios playing out in my head right now, but nothing makes sense. Just do us both a favor and tie me up," she said. "At least until we figure out what's going on."

"Quay, you just saved us from Regency capture. Clearly we're on the same side."

"I hope so," she said. "But until you can get me into Medical and find out where my life went, you can't take the chance that we aren't. They could've done anything to me: sleeper agent, doppelganger, maybe they filled me with a disease to spread to the rebels..."

She trailed off, her jaw sharp as a knife as she clenched against the fear rising in her. Finley said, "Okay, I'll take care of it."

She nodded. There was nothing else to say.

———

"Hey babe," Oscar said as he slipped into the copilot's seat. "I gave the prisoner the second dotal strip and his coughing is chilled."

Finley nodded. "What about Quay?"

"She's dosed and locked in the bunks."

Finley sighed. "I don't know if the sedation is really necessary."

"She thinks so."

"Either way, thanks for taking care of it."

Oscar put his hand on Finley's shoulder. "S'okay. I know you're a little squeamish. Besides, it gave me a chance to check some things." Oscar's smile melted to a grimace as he said, "I need to tell you something, and you're not gonna like it."

"I don't like a lot of things right now, so it can just mix in with the rest."

"Quay is truthy, far as I can see."

"You went digging?" Finley asked.

"Little. She's chipped, one of the oldies that don't keep a meshed log, but it still had some info."

"If it wasn't fully integrated, maybe it was faked," Finley said.

Oscar shook his head. "Nah. Even a primo hackbot couldn't match it so perfecto with the ship's logs."

"What did the ship say?"

"When I linked up, it was scattered. Thought it was thirty years ago and kept trying to update my software to its time. Then it could only give me nine months of data."

"You're hundred it couldn't have been altered?"

Oscar nodded. "There would be traces somewhere. One or other off by a nanosecond. But no, her chip matches the ship down to the tiniest snatch o' second. I'm hundred."

"I just don't see how it could be true."

Oscar shrugged. "I don't neither. Weird things, babe. Not the weirdest we've seen though, eh?"

Finley stared at Oscar, brows raised. "Yeah, mate, I think it is the weirdest. Some rando townie who used to fuck my dad shows up after missing the last however-long, saves us from Regency bounty hunters, then asks us to knock her out in case she's a sleeper agent—and you don't think that's the weirdest shit we've seen?"

Oscar shrugged. "'Member the rodeo on Panlucia?"

Finley flinched. "Okay, so this is the second weirdest. And we promised we wouldn't mention the rodeo ever again."

"Right, right," Oscar said. He looked at the passing blackness for a moment, seemingly lost in thought. Finally he shook his head and said, "I can't believe I didn't see it before. Fuck me, the rodeo saves us again."

"What are you talking about?"

"The brother-mucking Cloud Race, Fin. It's that all over again."

"Oscar, you're not making sense. Could you have caught a virus from the ship's computer?"

Oscar jerked back, offended. "This ship don't have the balls to try it. Knows my tech would scramble it perma."

"Then what are you saying?"

"I'm goin' in deep. Down to the day this ole heap o' metal was birthy."

"Anything I can do to help?"

Oscar stood and planted a kiss on Finley's forehead. "Check on me in an hour." He turned and stepped out of the cockpit. Before he turned around the hall's corner he yelled, "And make me a sandwich."

———

OSCAR WAS DIGGING FOR ELEVEN HOURS. FINLEY CHECKED ON him every hour, brought him food and water, but the food sat uneaten and the drinks still full. He tried talking to him, too, but Oscar was deep and couldn't hear him.

He went to Quay's room to check on her instead. She was out cold, sleeping through the sedation she'd demanded. Finley brushed the hair off her face and stared down at the strange woman, unsure what to make of her. It'd been less than a day, but he felt some sort of strange kinship with her. It wasn't attraction (at least he hoped it wasn't—that would put a strain on him, considering he'd never been attracted to a woman before), but it was some *need* to be around her, to help her, to love her.

"Blerg shit," he said, nearly jumping from the bed.

Love.

What a strange word to enter his head. He felt like he had a good grasp on the things around him, his feet grounded in reality. She flipped everything upside down. He walked up to the door, but couldn't stop himself from turning back to look at her again. She wasn't there. "What the—"

His words were choked off as an arm caught him around the throat. He pawed at the arm, but it held tight against him, closing off his air supply.

Quay's voice growled in his ear. "Who are you? How did you get on my ship?"

Despite her questions, she didn't ease up on her grip. Finley couldn't answer, could barely find a breath. Darkness closed in around the edges of his vision.

He slammed back against the wall, crushing her against it. Her grip tightened. He pounded against the wall, again and again. Quay wrapped her legs around him and strengthened her grip. Finley felt himself growing weaker, fell to his hands and knees on the ground.

Blessed air filled his lungs as her grip finally gave way. He sucked it in with great gulps, like a man with a bad spacesuit pulled inside just in time. He stared into Quay's green eyes as she lay on the floor beside him, a needle sticking from her neck. When his senses returned in full, he realized he had no idea what had happened.

Finley hated not knowing something. Made his brain itch.

He moved to get up and felt strong arms behind him, lifting him to his feet. Oscar spun him around, running hands over Finley's face and neck and hair before pulling him against his chest.

"I'm okay," Finley croaked. His voice was raw. He smiled, unable to stop himself. He sounded like one of those rugged cowboys on the movies his grandma liked (they were old when *she* was young).

"Only 'cause I came up when I did. If I'd stayed digging any longer, who knows?"

Finley pulled back a little, pressed his forehead against Oscar's. "But you didn't, and I'm okay. What about her?"

"Dosed her good. She'll be down a few hours."

"Thanks," Finley said. "Any idea what triggered her?"

Oscar frowned. "Sedatives? It's my only guess, though it doesn't make sense yet."

Finley slipped from Oscar's arms and they worked to tie

her up. This time, they checked her for sharp objects she could use to cut her ropes.

They headed toward the cockpit, Finley rubbing his sore neck the whole way. When they sat down, he asked, "Find anything from *The Quarrel*?"

A grin tore across Oscar's face. "It was buried, but yeah, I did. She might not remember the last twenty-seven years, but *The Quarrel* sure does."

"So the records are just sitting there?"

"Under layers of Regency security."

Finley drew a sharp breath. "Regency? Are you sure?"

Oscar shrugged. "Well, not exactly, but who else would it have been?"

Finley's mind raced, searching for an answer. The Regent was a fucker, no doubt about it, and his control of the planets made things difficult for the less than scrupulous (i.e. him and Oscar), but there was still plenty of life to be had under the radar. His control of the inner eight planets was tight; the planet-keepers who carried out his bidding had their own forces and were regularly reinforced with Regency troops, holding tightly to the requirements of the regime. But he wasn't as strict on the outer five. There were still keepers, sure (like that bastard, Duke MacReoch), and they were still richer than a Garovium mine on a warm day (when the Garovium was nice and melty and you could scoop it up with no effort, no machines, and no wasted fuel). Those outer keepers though, they let shit slide if it didn't suit them. And much of it didn't.

So why would the Regent, with all the control he already had, want to take some random woman and steal her life away? How did it benefit him to have Quay under his control? Was she a rebel? She certainly wasn't Regency...at least, not before she was captured thirty years ago. But she knew Finley's parents. How did they play into this?

Finley scrubbed a hand over his face, the questions too

taxing to think about in that moment. He said, "I don't know, but we need to find out. She didn't even remember me from a few hours ago. What else is she not remembering?"

"This ole trash pile's been flying around the whole time, even if she doesn't remember. The logs don't lie. Well, after you dig 'em up, anyway."

"So where has she been?"

"If she was with the ship, a whole lotta places. Through Doors that don't exist."

"Door Nine?"

Oscar nodded. "And ten, eleven, and twelve. Not to mention thirteen through twenty."

"Twenty?" Finley said, eyes widening.

"I thought it was a mistake, so I double-checked. And tripled. The coordinates are there."

"Holy shit," Finley whispered. "Twenty Doors. The Regent would *kill* for that intel."

"So would the rebels."

They stared at one another a moment, the words hanging in the air. Oscar was right. Anyone who discovered Quay's secret became a threat. The Regent would desire the Door coordinates to control trade in and out, and to make his volatile empire stronger. The rebels (and their dangerous, do-whatever-it-takes leader, Corelia Copal—great-grand-daughter of the overthrown original Regent) would use them to siphon control from the Regent as they had been trying, bit-by-bit, to do for the last hundred years.

After a moment, Finley looked up and said, "We're fucked."

Oscar nodded. "Well and truthy."

CHAPTER 3

inley watched the pale red planet grow in his vision. It was a nowhere-place, out beyond the invisible marker that divided the galaxy worth fighting for and the galaxy where neither Regent nor rebels gave two shits.

Streams of green swirled through the atmosphere, reminding him of the gas pools on Islington they had visited for their anniversary (a fun trip, until Oscar got arrested and Finley had his first run-in with the Dark Duke).

Oscar had erased every trace of what he'd found from the ship, after saving to his own tech, of course. There had been a fight about that. Finley had lost, obviously; Oscar was in charge of his own body, and despite Finley's objections because of the dangers, Oscar was going to do what he damned well pleased.

After the heated debate, followed by a furious make-up session, Finley found himself alone, staring at a planet he'd never thought to visit, looking for a Door he'd never known existed.

Footsteps rattled across the floor behind him and he heard Oscar let out a low whistle. "Foxy, in't she?"

"Why is it a she?"

Oscar shrugged. "Just is. Look at 'er."

Finley was. He'd been looking at her for a quarter of an hour as they made a slow approach into the atmosphere. No one had radioed, scans hadn't found anything, and she appeared empty. The planet seemed altogether perfect. Too much so.

"You think the prisoner would know anything?" Finley asked for the third time that hour.

Oscar sighed. "We've been over this."

"I know," Finley shrugged. "He's probably just a small-time bounty hunter hoping to make some credits by busting a couple Riders. But what if he isn't?"

"Whaddya thinkin'?"

"Maybe we were led to Nim-6 by those rumors as a way to draw out Quay."

"If she's Regency, why would they need to draw her out?"

Finley bit his bottom lip. "I don't know."

"And why us?" Oscar asked. "We're nobodies."

"She knew my dad. That's no coincidence."

Oscar shrugged. "Dunno. Seems like a few too many unknowns to make sense. Best we can do is get through Door Nine, like she wants. It's the one the ship logged more than any other. I just hope she don't kill us before we get there."

"Me too, Oscar. Me too."

———

THE AIR ON KYORL WASN'T BREATHABLE. THE GROUND (WHAT little they could find) was too soft to land on and kept eroding almost as soon as they found it. Water—or whatever the liquid was—swished back and forth under them, though neither could figure out what was controlling the ebb and flow.

Finley put the ship on auto and headed to the quarters. He wanted answers.

The coughing bounty hunter (who was also a certified heartthrob now that Finley could see him in proper lighting) they'd nabbed from the tavern was lying on the bed, black hair askew. His dark eyes opened lazily as Finley entered and a smirk passed across his lips, gone as quick as it came.

"I wondered when you'd come," he said.

"Don't be a gib," Finley said, rolling his eyes. "I'm not in the mood for it."

The man said, "What's wrong? Your other prisoner giving you trouble?" When Finley didn't respond, he asked, "She is your prisoner, right? Please tell me you're smart enough to figure that much out."

"What can you tell me about Magic Doors?" Finley asked, ignoring the man's jibes.

"Nothing you don't already know. Quay's the expert."

"What were you doing in the tavern?"

"Looking for my wife."

Finley blinked. It wasn't the answer he'd expected. "Your wife?"

"Yeah," the guy said. "I've been tracking her for months, got a lead she was there."

"But why was the Dark Duke there?"

"Hell if I know. I was there to see Shasta."

"Shasta."

The man raised his brows. "Tall, ponytail, probably dead now? Not ringing any bells?"

Finley remembered the crew in the alley. Quay *had* shot someone with a ponytail. "I remember."

The man lifted his tied hands from his lap as he talked. "Yeah, well, didn't really need Shasta when I saw Quay serving drinks. But then she poisoned me, so there's that."

The pieces clicked together in Finley's head. "You're Quay's husband?"

He nodded. "I guess so. Is there a certain number of times

a person has to try to kill you before you stop being their spouse?"

Finley floundered for a moment. "Uh, twelve?"

"Twelve? Hmmm. Is that for real or did you make it up?"

"Pretty sure it's twelve," Finley said, though he knew full well it was one.

"Damn. Guess I'm outta luck."

Finley put his hands on his cheeks and pressed until his lips puckered. Through fish-lips he said, "I'm so fucking lost."

The man chuckled. "Gets me now and then, too. Even when you know all the parts, it'll make your brain hurt. Has she tried to kill you yet?"

Finley nodded, and the man nodded along with him commiseratingly.

After a minute, Finley said, "So, you uh, wanna get a drink?"

———

ADGER OLIFELD WAS A GHOST. AT LEAST, THAT'S WHAT OSCAR'S records said. But he had an explanation for that: he was from a different galaxy.

"He's fork-feeding us a load of blerg shit," Oscar said.

They were outside the circular kitchen in the center of the ship. The door was open. Finley looked in to see Adger smiling at him and waving the plastic spoon they'd finally agreed to give him (after a heated debate on how likely it was he could kill them with it, including the death stats Oscar pulled up to use for his side of the argument), so he could eat his engorged protein pack (made with REAL air!).

Finley shrugged. "I dunno. I think I believe him. Call it a hunch."

"A hunch in your pants, maybe. Pretty boy fills your ears with crazy and you lap it up."

Oscar was right, he was pretty. His skin was a pale olive,

his features dark. He had just the right amount of stubble to be sexy without looking sloppy (a feat Finley had been trying —and failing—to master for years). He smiled when he should be angry, smirked when he knew he was right, and Finley could tell there was trouble brewing behind those dark eyes if he really wanted to let the storm go.

He didn't try to deny it. "He might heat the water, but it still boils at home."

Oscar rolled his eyes. He had never been the jealous type. He said, "Just try not to fuck up, k? Don't trust him, do not untie him, at least until we know more."

Finley nodded. "Speaking of, I should probably check on Quay and see if she can help sort some of this out."

"Good luck," Adger scoffed, confirming he was listening to the whole conversation.

"We can get them on their way and get back to siphoning from the rich, eh? Maybe we'll find some rare goods to smuggle from one of these Doors, make an assload of credits, and take a big vacation?"

Oscar frowned as Finley nudged him. Finally he said, "I want the whole thing this time. Flashy. No work while we're there."

Finley nodded. "As long as *you* promise not to get arrested this time."

Oscar smiled. He passed Finley and headed back toward the cockpit. "You know I can't promise."

Finley shook his head and sighed. He hoped he could deliver on a payload to get them away from this dangerous life.

But until then, he had the husband-and-wife-sized pain in his ass to deal with. He looked into the kitchen again. Adger gave him a wry smile and a wink.

———

Quay was awake when Finley entered the room. She was sitting on the bed, her eyes rimmed in red. Finley's heart hurt seeing her like this.

"Jack!" she yelled, jumping to her feet. She threw her tied hands around Finley's neck and kissed him hard on the mouth. When she pulled away, she was smiling. "I knew you'd rescue me. Thank Daya and her vengeful angels you're here."

Finley stared, mouth ajar. "I'm, uh, not Jack."

She pulled back and looked at him, her smile falling just a bit. "What are you saying? Of course you are. I'd know those eyes anywhere."

Finley pulled her arms up and off his neck. "Jack is my dad. I'm Garret."

Quay put her hands on top of her head. "It's happening again, isn't it?"

"What is?"

"Lonnia. Robert, then Jack. Now you."

"Lonnia and Robert?" Finley asked. "Robert Finley?"

She nodded.

"Please don't tell me you fucked my grandpa, too." She didn't respond, but Garret took it for a yes.

He pulled her arms from above her head and walked her to the kitchen. Adger was still there, spooning up the last of his food. "Hi, honey."

"No, no," she said, backing into Finley.

"What's wrong?" Finley asked.

"He's gonna take me back. He's gonna wipe it all out and take me back. I don't want to go."

Finley looked to Adger, who continued to smile up at Quay as she backed behind Finley. Finley asked, "What's she talking about?"

Adger shrugged. "She's been through a lot. I don't know how long she's been off her medicine. If we can get some into her, we might be able to make sense of it all."

"What medicine?"

"It's in my front pocket," Adger said. He pointed his chest toward Finley, offering the medicine to him.

Finley took two steps toward him, but Oscar's voice caught his attention and he stopped. He turned, trying to make out the words Oscar was yelling through the ship. Rope slid around his neck as something sharp jabbed into his side. Adger pulled the object out and Finley glimpsed the end of a plastic spoon chewed into a shiv.

Fuck me, he thought. *Now I'll have to tell Oscar he was right.*

Adger didn't stab him again. Instead, he threw Finley to the side and tore off after Quay. Oscar came around the corner a moment later, a grin on his face. "It's raining. The Door should show—what the hell?"

"Get to Quay," Finley said. He was already applying pressure to the wound on his side. He wasn't bleeding bad enough to die, as long as Oscar could patch him up soon, but he wasn't sure what Adger wanted with Quay. And they couldn't afford to find out.

"You're bleeding," Oscar said.

"He's trying to drug her. I dunno why. Save her. I can wait."

Oscar pressed his lips together and Finley knew he didn't want to leave him. But he did. Oscar always did what was right. Finley watched him leave the kitchen, heard the clatter of running feet, felt the shock of a pulse blaster going off. *Who was on the receiving end?*

He looked up through the small window in the kitchen's ceiling, blinking away tears and the ragged breaths that wouldn't stop. He could see the faint outline of a Door forming: darkness leaked out the edges, black as Arphilus ink, but inside was a comet-tail of colors arcing round and round, spinning so feverishly it was hypnotic.

Finley watched the colors spin and swirl, expand and contract, as they drew closer, pulled by the field of the Door.

He watched until he forgot about the others, forgot the blood pouring from his side, forgot his own name. He watched until the tears he was crying were from keeping his eyes open too long, until Oscar was a memory and Quay was a dream.

Then the blood loss (more than he had expected, actually) got the better of him and he passed out on the cold metal floor.

CHAPTER 4

"I know you don't understand," Adger said.

Finley turned his eyes toward the voice as he came awake. Adger was sitting in the pilot seat of *The Quarrel*, staring out into whatever was beyond. Finley straightened, adjusting in the co-pilot seat he was strapped to. It hurt to move, hurt to think through the fog in his brain, and it took him a moment to remember that he didn't like Adger.

Finley blinked a few times, trying to shake loose his thoughts. He said, "I understand. Mostly."

Adger scoffed. "Then maybe you can clear some of it up for me. Because there are parts I still don't get."

"Why are you after Quay?"

"I told you. She's my wife."

"Doesn't seem like she wants to be."

"Of course not," Adger said. "You're a Finley."

Garret furrowed his brows. "And?"

"She always loses her shit when she's around one of you. Some kind of marker in your blood, I think. Makes her chip malfunction and sends her spiraling."

"Okay, maybe I understand less than I thought," Finley said. He grunted as he tried to straighten up in his restraints.

"Sorry about the whole stabbing thing," Adger said. "I patched you up a bit. I didn't want to hurt you."

"Strange way to seal our friendship."

Finley's thoughts turned to Oscar. His head swiveled, looking for him, but he wasn't in the pit. The pulse that had gone off...

"I locked him up, but he's fine. Nearly pulsed my head off though," Adger said, rubbing his fingers through his thick hair.

They sat in silence a few minutes, staring off into the world below them. There were clouds, fluffy and golden, glowing under the double suns above them.

"Where are we?" Finley asked.

"Fosh," Adger said. "It's the second planet on the other side of Door Nine."

"This is what Quay was looking for."

"Yeah, I figured. She comes here just before the end."

Finley watched a flock of purple and silver birds fly under the ship. They were thick-necked with large heads and spindly wings that seemed to struggle to support them. Sink, swoop, repeat. Like people. They were beautiful.

"So she's what? A sleeper agent? A clone? Regency?"

"Yes. Damn, I didn't think you'd know all that. Makes it easier on me, honestly."

"Wait, what? She's all of them?"

Adger shrugged as if in apology, then flew below the clouds. Finley's eyes grew wide as he stared at rows and rows of...*something*. Glowing *something* for miles in each direction. With streams of black and pulsating green between them. Cables of some kind, he realized, as they got closer.

And then they were circling close enough for Finley to see bodies in the glowing *somethings*. Freezer-birth chambers, that's what they were.

Quay was in each one.

———

THEY LANDED ON A SMALL HILL IN THE CENTER OF THE FIELDS OF Quay. Finley followed Adger out of the ship. The air was breathable during the day, Adger told him, but at night noxious gasses released from the flora. Finley didn't see any flora, but Adger assured him it was there, hiding from the sun for the next few hours.

"She hates it here," Adger said as they walked through rows of Quay's forever-young face.

"But she was trying to get here."

Adger nods. "Something in her knows when the time is coming."

"The time?"

"To switch bodies," Adger said. He chuckled. "I guess this is where it gets complicated."

Finley stood over a Quay as she looked up through sightless eyes. "What is she?"

"She's Perian Quay, the love of my life. She's also on the fourth version of that woman."

"Why is she like this?"

"She sought immortality and her lead scientist provided it."

"So she *is* Regency."

"She's not just Regency," Adger said, "she's the Regent. The original that started it all. That's why the current Regent is so desperate to find her. If she remembered everything, she could destroy him."

"I'm lost," Finley said. "It's too fucking much."

Adger nodded. "Tell me about it. Try being married to her."

"So she was the first regent from a hundred and some years ago. She made herself immortal by switching into a new body when the old…what? Wears out? But at the cost of her memory."

"Kinda. She remembers the most when she first wakes. That's always the best for us. We can go home and enjoy life for a few years. But after a while, she starts to forget things. Little things, at first. Then me," Adger said, his voice cracking.

Finley winced. He couldn't imagine what it would be like to lose Oscar over and over and still be trying to keep it together. "I'm sorry."

"It's fine. I mean, it's not, but you know. Do what you have to for the one you love."

"What happens after, you know, she forgets?"

"She goes looking for a Finley."

Garret squinted, confused. "But why?"

"You're what she remembers from before me and she goes retracing her steps. She forgets about the clones and who she was, and searches for the last thing she knew before the gap in her memory."

"My grandpa?"

"Great-grandpa," Adger says, smirking. "Rutger Finley was the one she loved before she was Regent. When she went haywire the first time, long before I knew her, she went looking for Rutger and found his daughter, Lonnia, instead. She loved her, too. Your grandpa Robert was the third Finley, then your dad, last time, and now you."

"You said it was a marker in our bloodline?"

Adger shrugged. "It's just a guess. Something keeps pulling her back. She can somehow find you, no matter where you are."

Finley sighed. Part of him felt like he could understand what Adger was saying. He'd felt pulled to Quay from the moment he saw her. There was a need in him to protect her, and it wasn't something he understood or knew how to explain. How did you tell her husband you loved her, even though you'd just met? How did you explain it to yourself? Oscar would understand—it wasn't the same as the love he had for him, after all, it was more rooted, like he'd always had it buried inside him but didn't know until he saw her.

He turned to look at the ship in the distance, realizing how far they'd walked. He turned back to Adger to ask where they were going, but found Adger pointing a blaster at him instead.

Adger motioned for Finley to raise his hands as he said, "I'm really sorry about this, fella. It wasn't the plan."

Finley got a sick feeling in the pit of his stomach. "Oscar isn't in quarters, is he?"

Adger swallowed, shook his head almost imperceptibly. "I'm truly sorry about that, Finley."

That was it then. Without Oscar, there wasn't much point to life. Smuggling and outrunning the Regency? It was boring without that white-eyed wonder by his side.

"What happens now?" Finley asked. "You gonna fly off with a new Quay?"

Adger shook his head. "Nah, I think I'm done with that life."

"You're just going to let her die?"

"No, of course not. I'm going to turn her in."

Finley's jaw dropped. This man claimed to love her, but he knew with every fiber of his being that he would've done anything to save Oscar, to spare him from pain. Love wouldn't allow him to turn Quay in to the Regency, so clearly he didn't love her.

"Don't give me that look," Adger said. "Sad eyes aren't gonna sway me. I'm too tired of racing around the Doors for a woman who will always forget me."

Adger backed away from Finley, still pointing the blaster at his chest. As he went, he began pressing buttons on a gadget on his wrist. All around them, birther pods began to open. The Quays inside didn't move, still asleep without the chip that held Quay's memories and personality.

"The gas," Finley said, his mouth going dry. "You're going to kill her."

"She's already dead," Adger said. "These are just copies."

Finley took a step toward him and Adger fired a warning shot at his feet. "Don't move again. I don't want to shoot you."

Finley laughed. "Go ahead. You've already taken away the only thing I've ever loved. And you're leaving me here to die anyway!"

"Good point," Adger said.

His finger pressed the trigger. A jet of red shot Finley in the chest and he dropped to the ground. He listened as the remaining pods opened, as Adger footsteps faded away, as he started up the ship. He saw the craft pass overhead, followed by a flock of birds, dark spots against the twilight sky.

The suns had set, leaving Finley in the dark of Fosh. He heard a rustle and turned his head to the left. Pushing up through the ground was a vibrant green plant with shimmery white veins.

"Aren't you foxy?" Finley mumbled.

He heard a hiss, and saw the air above him alight with sparkling particles floating toward the ground. A cough tickled his throat as he closed his eyes.

AS CONSTANT AS
UNSEEN STARS

Originally published in *Post Apocalipstick*

CHAPTER 1
AS CONSTANT AS UNSEEN STARS

My mask has a hole in it. It's small, almost invisible, but I taste the air seeping in. It will kill me if I don't fix it. I catch Arden's eye and point at my mouth. She nods, packs her tools, and moves toward the pit.

"What's up?" Juniper's voice comes through my headset with its trademark sweetness.

"Lark's mask is shit," Arden says. "But don't worry, I've got a replacement."

"New?" Juniper asks.

"Nah," Arden laughs. "I'm gonna Frankenstein this bitch."

"You're awfully quiet," Juniper says.

"She has to be, Jun. Her mouthpiece is compromised. Can't risk pulling in more air."

Damn it, I think. Arden should know better than to say something like that to my sister.

"Good thing it's such as easy fix," Malijah says, her clipped tone cutting through my earpiece.

I'm glad Mal knows how to keep Juniper calm. I glance in my mirror as she comes into view, give her a nod, though I don't know if she sees me. The land-crawler is speeding across the terrain, bumping and jumping as we go, and it makes it hard to read each other's movements.

Arden takes the hint and says, "O' course. Breezy, boss."

Mal says, "I'll man the gun so you can fix her."

I swivel my gun toward the front of the crawler. Malijah kisses two fingers and taps the ice cream on the side of the truck—a good luck tradition for climbing the crawler. Watching her maneuver out of the pit and up the plank, jumping into the engine cage and then the switchback walkway that leads to my gun, well, it's a thing of beauty. She is the most graceful woman I've ever seen, encased in the most terrifying person I've ever known.

I scan the horizon once more before Mal reaches me, though it's been empty for days. My eyes skim over the red wild to our right. The smog is heavy and I can't see far, but I'm not worried about anything coming from there. No one lives in the red wild—no one can. It's a wasteland.

There are mountains on our left; hills, really, but it makes my sister happy to think of them as the mountains in the old stories, so I go with it. You could cross them with a jacked-up crawler on the right wheels, but I'm not worried about that either. Anything that could cross the hills would be heard long before it found us.

Malijah steps into the cage and I give her my seat. Arden's already sliding through the window into the pit. I wrap my hand on the railing and scamper down the first plank to the engine. I've been begging for a ladder to climb straight down from the gun into the ice cream truck, but it would compromise the integrity of the pit. So instead I cross the rickety switchback, terrified of falling at these speeds, though I'll never admit it to the others.

I'm about to drop to the lower plank when I hear an engine revving. My head jerks up and I spin toward the sound. There's a bullet, a two-seated crawler, coming up behind us, moving too fast. *Dangerously* fast.

Then it hits me: they're not alone.

No one is stupid enough to approach another vehicle out here, unless they're starting a road war. And a tiny thing like that has backup or they'd stay away.

I climb back up toward the gun. Malijah spots me and her voice slams into my headset. "What the fuck, Lark? Go get your mask fixed. I can handle the bullet."

I slip behind her and grab the noculars. The bullet will be on us in seconds, but I'm not concerned about them. I scan the smog, praying I'm wrong. Nothing on the road, nothing by the hills. *Fuck me.*

"There's a roller comin' from the red," I say.

A cough overtakes me before the words are all the way out. I grab Malijah's shoulder and pull her from my chair. The gun is *mine* and she knows it. They all do. I'm damn good with it—in fact, it's the only thing I'm good at.

Mal's voice comes over the headset, calm, steady. "Arden, wake up Prue. Put them on spikes and tar. See if you can cobble some tech that won't leave us short for the battle for Safety. Jun, you're the best damned driver I know. Do what you can."

We both know what she needs from me and I've already spun to face the roller. Even without the words, I can hear what she's thinking: Don't speak.

I have time, as long as I don't draw too much air through the mouthpiece.

I hold up the noculars for another look. I recognize the gunner, though not by name. He was top three last year. I can't imagine how shitty it feels to get that close and then not make it in. I've never made it past the lottery. That's a different kind of shitty.

Covering my mouth with my hand, I say, "Top three gunner on the roller."

The scrape of metal on metal fills the space around me. I don't look. Whatever's happening with the bullet has nothing to do with me. My eyes stay glued to the roller lurching toward us.

It's massive; an old dump truck, from the look of it. The back has been covered with sheets of metal, a gun cage stuck on the top. There are small holes along the sides just big enough to use small arms if they can get them. The cab has been reinforced with metal bars so that only a thin strip of sight-space is usable for the driver—so narrow, even *I* couldn't get a shot through while the thing's moving. Each side of the cab has another gun, unmanned, for now.

Rollers aren't known for their speed. Most are too bulky to be fast, but this one is quicker than usual. We could outrun it on a short haul, but not if we're going to make it to Safety. We're two days out and already unsure if we're going to have enough fuel to get there.

Movement at the corner of my eye catches my attention. Someone from the bullet has boarded us. They're hanging onto the bar that runs past the engine. Before I can warn the others, I see Malijah headed toward them with a crowbar in one hand and a pistol in the other. I hope she can hit him without using the gun. She's a terrible shot.

People are lined up on the side of the roller with hooks and ropes. They don't want to destroy us—they want to board us.

Fuck that.

I take aim at their gunner. If I can take him out, we might have a chance. On a roller that big, there are probably back-ups. We've got five on our crawler; that monstrosity could fit twenty.

But the other nineteen are nothing to me. I only need to take out this one.

"You got aim?" Malijah asks.

"Yeah." I hope she doesn't hear the relief in my voice that she's okay. I don't need her thinking I *care* about her.

"The bastards got one aboard. Don't let them get another."

With those words, I shoot. Their gunner goes down easy and I shift my aim to the roller's side. I'm three shots in before they notice their comrades falling. As they move for cover, I find an exposed leg and nick someone else, but the simple shots are gone.

The roller backs off and puts some space between us— enough that I can't pick them off. Through the noculars I see all three of their guns fill up, but I'm not worried. If I can take out a top three with such ease, those asshats won't be a challenge.

"White flag," Mal says.

No way, I think. *It's a trap.*

"It's clearly a trap," Malijah says.

I smile. Damn that woman for being so smart. If she's not careful, I'm going to end up telling her how sexy she is.

We don't slow, and soon I hear the roller's engine resume its speed. I train my gun on their front gunner. As soon as they get close enough—

Crack!

Our crawler teeters for a second and my gun is thrown off balance. My seat swivels too far left and I lose sight of their gunners while I struggle to regain my balance. I cough into my headset, "What the fuck?"

"Sorry," Juniper comes back. "I was trying to dodge the bullet and side-swiped a tree."

Tree? I think. I glance over my shoulder and see that we have indeed crossed into the forested lands. I'd be thrilled to see them if it wasn't for people trying to murder us.

I've finally got my gun back in line, but the roller is almost on us. Their gunners are firing against our side. I hear it, now that I'm listening—the *ping* of bullets coming against the steel reinforcements. Our bitch can handle a gun or two, with all the work we've done to her.

I take aim at the left gunner and shoot. Kill shot, right between the eyes. The second gunner hits the floor. He's still firing, but recklessly, without sight. That may be worse than when he was shooting our side. I fire in his direction and I must hit him, because his gun ceases. The roller closes in and I take aim at the third.

Fire burns across my temple, a shitstorm of pain. I scream, sucking in air, and throw myself to the ground as coughing wracks my body. That bastard shot me! I press one hand against my mask and hold it to my face while trembling fingers prod the side of my head. They come away bloody. *Really* fucking bloody. Not only did the asshole slice the side of my head, they ripped the strap of my breather. I'll have to hold it to my face to live; makes it hard to fire a two-hander when you need one hand to breathe.

"Lark!" Jun yells.

I don't answer, though I know she'll be worried sick until I do. I've already consumed more pollution today than the yearly allowance. I roll to my stomach and crawl toward the gun. I may not be able to use it fully, but at least I can signal that I'm okay. I reach for the railing to pull myself up. A bullet rips into the metal beside me and I jerk my hand back.

Their gunner is good, probably second to the first I killed. Really they should be thanking me. I moved them up a position.

If I can't get to the gun, I'm useless. Maybe I can help inside. I crawl a few feet to the edge of the cage. I'm gonna have to drop onto the plank and make a run for it. I pull myself into a crouch and take a deep breath.

One.

Two.

The roller crashes into the side of us, throwing me against the back of the gun cage. I can feel Jun trying to shake them off, braking and gassing in alternate patterns, but they're moving us now.

The clang of their hooks hitting the side of our crawler

clinks in my ears. They're boarding us. Fuck me. If they board us, we're done. There's only one option.

I dive behind the gun, hoping their gunner is distracted. They're not, and the *ping* of bullets hits around me. But they're careful to avoid the gun. *Obviously, fuckface. A gun like this is hard to come by. They want my baby.*

Taking a deep breath of air through my nose, I hold it, then drop my mask and use both hands to swivel the beast around. I lay waste to the boarders, shooting without aim, hoping to hit them anywhere. A few fall back, but most fall down, hit by my barrage of bullets.

Two make it on the crawler. Malijah is on them in an instant. I'd love to watch her take them down because: a. She's some kind of sexy, violent sorceress with her fists and b. I wanna know she's safe. But instead I'm scrabbling around the area where my mask should be. My lungs are starting to burn now; tiny pinpricks of fire sing inside me, begging for another gulp of air, poison or not.

"Looking for this?"

A stranger stands by the engine, dangling my mask with one finger. I dive toward them, knowing I don't have much time. Bastard must've boarded earlier, after I got shot. And if *one* did…

A scream slices the air.

"Juniper," I breathe, forgetting my mask and the air and the boarder. My vision tunnels until all I can see is the cab of the crawler, two forms grappling inside.

I jump up, startling the boarder. I barrel my fist into their throat and when they double over coughing, I rip off their mask and put it on myself. They cry out, shoving my broken mask against their face as coughing overtakes them. In their panic, they seem to forget I'm there. Until I kick my boot into their chest and they fall backwards off the crawler, clanging down the metal side before getting smashed against a tree.

I drop onto the plank and in three long strides I'm at the

pit. I climb the rungs to the cab, slide the cover to the side, and hurl myself toward Jun. I jump on the back of the boarder who has her pinned to the wall, wrapping my arm around his throat. I squeeze with all my might, relishing the moment he releases Jun and focuses on me. He throws himself against the wall, pinning me against it and knocking the breath from my lungs.

But I hold steady. Again and again he pounds us against the wall, my head smacking against the metal. I know there's blood but I don't let go, my forearm snug against his throat. The boarder stops struggling, stops slamming us into the wall, stumbles. He moves, slowly, toward the window and propels us through. We fall and I know I'm going to die.

I BLINK AGAINST THE GRAY LIGHT. MY BRAIN IS FOGGY. BUT I SEE Jun sitting in the shadows.

Blink.

And I see Malijah with her, holding my sister against her chest.

Blink.

And I see Mal stroking her cheek, kissing away her tears.

I leave my eyes closed this time and drift back into unconsciousness, back into the sweet oblivion that lets me forget that my sister was kissing the woman I love—that the woman I love seems to love my sister.

I'M ALONE WHEN I OPEN MY EYES AGAIN. IT'S DARK HERE. AS MY eyes adjust to my surroundings, I realize I don't know where *here* is.

I sit up and immediately regret it. Pain surges through my head as the blood rushes in. I grip my head in my hands to hold myself steady. When the spinning stops and I'm moderately confident I can keep my balance, I stand. I feel along the walls—I can reach them simply by stretching out my arms in the small space—until I find what constitutes a door. I slide it open.

Light and heat and noise rush in and I hear Jun's laugh and my stomach drops to my feet. Wherever we are, whatever happened, my sister is okay.

"You're gonna have a gnarly scar," a low voice says.

I turn toward the voice and let my eyes roam over the most handsome person I've ever seen. He's kicked back with his leg propped on a table and his head against the metal wall behind him. He looks up at me with eyes the brown of dead leaves, peeking from under unruly black curls. He's barechested, with a jagged scar under each nipple. A home-job, probably, since real doctors are nothing more than myth anymore.

My eyes linger on his scars unintentionally. He says, "You done?"

"Sorry," I mutter.

His lip curls into a sneer. "Not the first time."

I shake my head. "No excuse."

"True," he says. "But I'm gonna give you a pass since you had your head bashed in."

I laugh, surprising myself. "Thanks."

"Hudan," he says, holding out his hand.

"Lark!" Juniper yells. She bounds down the metal steps in the adjoining room. Jun wraps her arms around me from behind and rests her head against my shoulder. "I was so worried."

"Happy to see you, too," I say.

"I was about to fill Lark in on what she missed. Probably better if you do, though, eh?" Hudan gives a wink and says, "Welcome to my rig, babe."

Juniper takes my hand and pulls me up the metal steps.

We're in the top portion of a crawler of some sort, surrounded by caged in windows that let beams of light in. The sight of my sister in sunlight, without a mask—

"Fuck, Jun, where's our masks?"

She smiles. "The whole inner area of Hudan's crawler is air-controlled, with an airlock and everything. He rescued us after the roller attack. It's amazing. Right, honey?"

Malijah steps into the room behind us. Something about her seems off, *shy* even. Very un-Mal. She scrubs a hand over her freshly-shorn hair as if she's searching for words that aren't there. "Yeah, Juni, it's good."

"What's wrong?" I ask.

I know Mal—the crinkle by her eyes when she's hiding something, the way the corners of her lips turn down when she's upset. Something is wrong.

"It's Arden," she says. "She didn't make it."

A brick drops onto my chest. Arden has been with us for three years, side-by-side in the crawler every damn day. She's the best techie I've ever seen. She *was* the best techie. Now she's dead. I can't say anything about her, can't ask, so instead I force out, "Prue?"

"They're fine. Banged up a bit, but okay."

I nod. There are other questions, other things I need to know, things we need to figure out before we get to Safety, but it can wait. Right now, I just want a drink. I slip from Jun's grasp, push past Mal, ignore them both when they call after me. Instead I go back to Hudan, to the dimple in his chin, the trail of hair leading down his stomach, the curve of his hips as he lounges against the wall.

He looks up with a question in his eyes, but we both know the answer. He picks up a bottle of brown and takes my hand, leading me off to take comfort in the clean air in my lungs, in the salty sweat on my skin, in every little thing that lingers while I'm alive.

———

WE REACH SAFETY THE NEXT DAY. I HAVEN'T SPOKEN TO JUN OR Mal since I heard about Arden; it's not that I don't want to, it's that I can't. Her death is too close, too *real*, and only serves to remind me of the other lives we're risking by going to Safety.

We're parked outside the walls, of course, but close enough that I can see them from the cracks in the plates of metal lining Hudan's bedroom. I still can't believe he has his own room. What a fucking luxury.

He's lucky, he tells me, because his family was wealthy before things went to shit. They saw what was coming and built a compound for their family, with good air and supplies for fifty years. Those years came and went, and things only got worse. So Hudan's dad began working on their crawler. The compound was abandoned before Hudan was born, so his home has always been inside the metal walls.

"How did I end up here?" I ask, tracing my fingers along the scars on his chest.

I tilt my head up to see his half-smile; it's a crooked thing that would look ridiculous on any other face, but on his, it's perfect.

"My turn to get lucky," he says.

I frown at his double entendre. "I'm serious."

His brow creases. "We saw the smoke. If I'm being honest, I normally don't interfere in road wars. Nobody bothers us because of our size, so I figure it's best not to risk getting involved and showing our weaknesses."

"Why was this time different?"

He sighs. "They wanna rob you, fine. They want to kill you? Not my business. But you don't remove someone's mask and watch them choke to death. It's sick. So when I saw that..."

I swallow hard. *He saw them do that to Arden.*

He continues, "They ran when we approached. We weren't planning to help, just scare them off, but then, well, your sister got to me."

I smile, knowing exactly what he means. "She does that."

"She's worried about you," he says. I roll my eyes, but he says, "Seriously. You should talk to her."

I'm crawling from his side and looking for my clothes before the words are out of his mouth. Not because I'm going to go talk to Juniper, but because I don't need a lecture from the stranger I grief-fucked.

He watches me dress and the silence stretches between us, a chasm between people who don't know each other enough to bridge the gap. I reach for the door, and without turning back I say, "Thanks. You know, for this."

There's a low chuckle and he says, "Anytime."

———

THERE'S A ROW OF MASKS HANGING BY THE AIRLOCK. I GRAB ONE and step inside, wait for the lights to go green, and walk out into a gray afternoon. Mal is there, leaning against the crawler, and I consider going the opposite direction before she sees me. But of course that's stupid, because she already knows I'm there. She always does.

"It's a shitshow, Lark."

Her voice over my earpiece is a strange comfort, though I don't know what she's talking about at first. I follow her gaze to the grounds spread out before us and it's not hard to figure it out. Rows of rollers, crawlers, bullets, dozers, tankers, and cruisers are lined up as far as I can see. Every one of them is here for the same reason: to win entry into Safety.

It's the same sight every year, so I'm not sure what she's annoyed with. The annual pilgrimage is as constant as the unseen stars in the sky. There's no doubt as to why we make the journey every year; we all want to breathe, to live, and Safety is the only place for that.

They say it was a military base. I don't know or care if that's true. I care about the air filtration system that lets them walk around without the masks. I care about the dome overhead that protects their crops. Crops! They can grow *real* food, like the stuff we've only read about. Mostly I care about crossing that wall and seeing my mother and asking that bitch how she could leave her children. I was eleven, Juniper was eight, and our world went dark the day she crossed into Safety.

If she crossed. I've never said it aloud, never in front of Jun, but I always wondered if she died in the death match and no one had the heart to tell us the truth. Though honestly, thinking her dead might be easier than thinking she abandoned us.

"How long until the lottery?" I ask.

"Six hours," Mal says. "Need to find a fifth by then."

"No extras with Hudan?"

She shakes her head, pats the side of the crawler. "Shameful, to be riding around in this monster with only five people."

I look up at the thing, taking in the size of it. It's not something you notice inside, but now that she's said it I can't disagree. I think of his words and find my lips curling with the hint of a smile. "I guess we were lucky it was only five. He had room for us."

She looks at me and I watch her brows furrow. She puts a hand on my shoulder and I want to shake it away, I want it to stay—fuck—I don't know what I want. She says, "You can't trust him, Lark. You know that."

I nod. "Yeah. 'Course I know." I start to move away, let her hand drop off my shoulder. I've walked a few feet, but still close enough that my radio is in range. I say, "Remember though, there was a time we thought the same about you."

I don't give her a chance to respond, moving out of earshot. The market is set up a few rows over and I head there to take a look at the goods. They're lined up by type: gunner, strategist, arms, techie, and driver. I find the techies and walk the line, summarily unimpressed with what I see.

We don't *need* a fifth to compete, but since we're allowed to take five into Safety, why not give someone else a chance? I've watched winning teams with only one or two left alive choose to rescue strangers from the crowd at random; then again, I've also seen people go in alone.

At the end of the line, I'm about to turn around and walk it again, when a kid sitting in the dirt catches my attention. He's got a round face, doughy. There's a tool in one hand and a mask in the other, his eyes trained on his work as he ignores the shoppers.

I nudge him with my foot, hold up four fingers. He flicks his radio to the channel and I say, "Hey, kid, what's your deal?"

He looks annoyed that I'm talking to him. "My deal?"

"Yeah. Why are you here?"

He shrugs. "Nothin' else to do."

"You're young."

"Really?" he asks, looking wide-eyed at his arms. "I had no idea. Thanks for the info."

I smile. Gotta love a smartass. "Family?"

"Dead," he shrugs. "Yours?"

"Same, mostly."

We sit in silence for a minute before I start to walk away. I make it a few yards before I look back to see him following. When we get back to the crawler, Mal gives a curious look at him and I say, "We've got a new techie."

THE LOTTERY IS DRAWN AT SUNDOWN. HUDAN'S CREW IS THE sixth called. Delight and fear, joy and panic—they dance across his face in a strange pattern I can't fully understand. I am happy for him, truly happy that he has this chance to enter Safety, but there is also a pit of envy cramping my gut. I want my crew, my family, to have the same opportunity—

But then we do.

Malijah's name comes across the speakers in a monotone that somehow breathes color into my heart. We're in the match.

Hudan shakes hands with Mal, congratulating her, before stepping in front of me. His lips quirk up in that stupid grin and he says, "Try not to die."

I open my mouth to make a wisecrack, but find my voice is missing. Hudan nods as if he understands and moves to rejoin his crew. I turn and watch the joyful faces of mine, trying not to mourn them while they're still alive.

———

AT DAWN, THE TEN TEAMS ARE LINED ACROSS THE FIELD IN identical buggies. Each five-person craft is gassed up and loaded with the same equipment, plus each person can bring one personal item. We'd practiced with ours for months to make sure we had the right combination of things. But thanks to the roller, we go in without any.

I could probably forgive them for stealing our crawler and all our shit if it wasn't for what they did to Arden. It also doesn't make it easier when I see *my* gun in the hands of some prick three buggies down the line. Mal won't let me go take it back, even after the asshole catches my gaze and blows me a kiss.

Instead, we battle. The arena is nothing more than clean ground in a makeshift circle, surrounded by the crawlers who didn't make the lottery. Their teams stand at the edge, cheering and drinking and pretending there will be a chance for them next year.

Our only goal is to be the last buggie moving. Knock the others out, bust their buggie, kill them, whatever.

Juniper whips us through spaces we ought not fit and my chest fills with pride at her ability. Gunners and arms are the positions most praised, but you can't do shit without a good driver.

I fire off the standard gun at the tires of a couple competitors, but it doesn't do much. This gun might as well be a water-pistol for all the good it's doing. But it doesn't matter, because Jun is keeping us going and nothing has been able to hit us so far.

We come face to face with Hudan. Neither of us fire. We pass in understanding, in truce, and some vague point in my chest leaps with this fact. I tuck it away to dissect later, when we're not courting death.

A spray of bullets hits the side of our buggie and I spin to find my gun trained on us. *Ain't that some shit.* But he isn't familiar with her tricks and he's managed to smack himself in the face. I want to laugh; instead, I lift my piddling gun and take aim at his head. I shoot, and I've already aimed at their driver when the gunner slumps over. The driver follows. Their buggie spins out of control and tips over. I know they're out of the running, but I can't help myself, not when Arden's smile enters my mind. I pop off their techie, their arms, and finally, gleefully, their strategist. There will never be another Arden dead on the side of the road, at least, not by their hands.

When I look up, there are only four teams left. "Holy fucking shit," I scream. "We can do this!"

Our techie kid whips away a bomb he's been toiling with. It misses the bug he's aiming for and rolls toward the edge of the crowd. They scramble away from it as he shrugs and says, "Oops."

The next he throws explodes under one of the bugs and suddenly there are only three of us left. Top three. There's a chance…

When Prue's head whips back and she slumps down, my insides go cold. Malijah is yelling something over the radio, but I can't make out the words. The kid does, though, because he tackles me, landing on top. The buggie skids and we're rolling across the field. I can't see Juniper, but I'm certain she's dead.

We stop rolling and I try to push the kid off me. He doesn't move. I slip out from under him and find the back of his head bloody. I didn't even know his name. I stumble out of the buggie and rush to the front, to Jun. She's slumped over the steering wheel, and her head is bleeding, but she's breathing.

Malijah is waking up beside her. She mumbles, "Hide."

It takes me a second to realize what she means. Maybe they'll kill us like I killed the roller people. I look to the field in panic, but only one team remains.

It's over.

———

HUDAN, HIS SISTER, AND HER CHILD ARE PACKING THEIR belongings when we stumble back to the crawler. As soon as he sees me, Hudan pulls me against his chest and whispers, "I'm glad you made it."

I laugh against his ear, feel the bitterness of it. "Yeah, thanks."

I push away from him, but he holds my arm and whispers, "We have two spots. You and your sister."

I pull back and look at him. He lost two. But his eyes are excited and I feel my heart beat wildly for this man I barely know. He's going to save us.

I turn to Jun. And Malijah. My heart sinks back to where it

was before. I lean into Hudan and whisper in his ear. His brow furrows, but he nods and goes upstairs.

"We're going to meet Hudan in the alcove for a goodbye drink," I say.

Jun gives a nod and heads that way. I grab Mal's arm as she passes and say, "Two spots, Mal. But you're going to have to help me, because she won't do it any other way."

Malijah's eyes go wide as understanding dawns on her face. "No way. Not happening."

"Don't fight, Mal. I'm making the best call for my sister."

"She needs you."

I shake my head. "She'll never forgive me, no matter who stays behind. At least this way I can save you, too."

She doesn't speak, but her honeyed eyes tell me all the words she cannot say. She *knows*. All this time without telling her how I felt, and she already knew. She moves away and my hands fall numb at my sides as I watch her head after Jun. I follow a few steps behind, trying to steady myself for what I'm about to do.

I stop, staring at Jun bathed in sunlight. I try to memorize each line of her face, the curve of cheekbone and slope of her nose. She waves me over and the smile on her face almost melts my resolve. My little sister, twenty years old, sweet and unbreakable.

Hudan hands me a glass and I clink it against Juniper's. We down our drinks and smile at one another. I say, "Juni, Hudan has two open spots."

Her eyes go to him and he nods. She beams for a moment, then breaks as she looks between Mal and me. I continue, "He's taking you and Mal."

"What about you?" she asks.

"I'm going to build a new team. I'll see you next year."

"No," she says. "If you're staying, so am I."

"There's no guarantee, love," Mal says.

I hear a softness in Mal's voice that I've never heard

before. I wondered what it would sound like, that sweetness that only unravels with intimacy. I've never managed to hear it for myself.

"I don't care. I'm not going without you."

I take her hand in mine and press it against my cheek, relishing our last moments. "I knew you'd say that. That's why I spiked your drink."

Her other hand grasps at the table as she starts to go. "Lark, I…" she mutters, but she's out now.

Mal picks her up and carries her down the steps, following Hudan's family. I trail behind them, unsure of myself.

Mal says, "I love you, Lark. I hope you know that."

My heart hammers, but all I can manage is, "Take care of her."

She nods and heads into the airlock. I watch Jun as the door slides closed, seeing her for the last time.

Hudan lingers. "I wish I could stay."

"I know," I say, though really, I don't know why he would consider it.

"You're somethin' else, babe. Find me when you make it over." He tosses me the keys to his crawler and steps out into the airlock without another word.

From the bird's nest in the top of the crawler, I watch them cross the field with the noculars Hudan left behind. I watch them ride the lift up the wall. I watch Jun wake up halfway, Mal and Hudan holding her arms as she fights against them.

They're almost at the top when Jun stops fighting. She holds a hand up in farewell. They'll be waiting for me, my family. And someday I will get there.

HILLBILLY NECROMANCER: A LOVE STORY

Originally published in *Bad Romance* by Black Hare Press

CHAPTER 1

HILLBILLY NECROMANCER: A LOVE STORY

Johnny P. Nash was waist deep in grave dirt for the second time in a week. He leaned over his shovel and took a deep, unsteady breath. The misty air was cold, burning his lungs as he gulped it in.

He felt old. In truth, he was only in his early forties; but the years were long, many of them unkind, and forty-three was feeling like a ripe old age to his bones. He was certainly too old to be digging up bodies in the middle of the night.

Johnny took a swig of piss-whiskey—moonshine made by the finest distiller in Logan County—and coughed until he hacked up a fine wet loogie. He sighed and dipped his shovel into the dirt again.

Hasn't always been like this, he thought.

And it hadn't. Once he had owned the largest Necromancy center in all of southern West Virginia. Clients as far as Morgantown, down past Pikeville, and even the fancy coal barons living like kings in Charleston had sought his help.

Now, though, he served the eccentric widow or grieving father for pennies on the dollars he used to make. He took his pay in homemade biscuits or pepperoni rolls, a ride to town his truck broke down, an invitation to hear some down-home Bluegrass at the park.

Johnny spit, puckered up his lips. He always felt sour when he was digging up the dead. Maybe that was the only way you could feel.

His shovel clanged against something below. He scraped against the dirt, freeing up the edge of the coffin. Johnny dropped to his knees and began scooting the dirt away from the opening. When it was clear, he opened the casket and stared down at the young man within.

Most of him was still there, certainly enough to revive for a night out on the town. But in all fairness, Johnny could bring them back with only a bag of bones. He was good, damn good, and no dead body was going to best him.

He stood up, stretched his aching muscles, and pulled his toolbox toward the hole. Johnny withdrew his tools: two bottles with liquids in them, an eyedropper, a Ziploc baggie full of shiny black powder, and a spray can of axe body spray. Many a client had trouble with the smell of a decomposing body, so Johnny had taken to bringing the spray along to help mask the decay with something only slightly less offensive.

He lined his items in a neat row along the side of the grave (he'd always believed that ninety percent of being a good Necromancer was organization) and proceeded to voodoo the life back into—he looked up at the tombstone, then confirmed the name written in sharpie on his dirty left hand—Mikey Bowyer. Johnny smiled. At least the names matched this time.

He waited.

Sometimes the dead weren't too happy about being brought back to life, so Johnny always stayed until he saw that they were behaving. His will over them would hold for a while, but he liked to tell his customers it was a one night only affair. It helped them let their loved ones go a little easier or left those wanting to see them longer more willing to pay for the extra time.

The Bowyer boy twitched. About time. Johnny hoped to

get a few hours of sleep before the sun came up. The body began to move in the coffin and after a moment he sat up.

"Howdy kid, I'm Johnny P. Nash. I just raised you from the dead and I'm your master. Any questions?"

"Braaaaaaains," the boy said.

Johnny took a step back. Well, that was odd. He hadn't turned someone into a zombie since that little boy in '94. What a fucking mess.

"BRAAAAAAAINS," he said, climbing up from the casket and reaching toward Johnny.

"Guess I'll be sending you back then. No zombies on my watch."

The boy's arms dropped and he stopped his forward motion. "Oh gosh, Mr. Nash, don't send me back yet. I'd like to visit Maw before I'm dead again."

"Well what's with all the 'braaaains' bullshit?" Johnny asked, raising his hands to imitate the boy.

Mikey shrugged. "I just thought it'd be funny. Like a movie, you know?"

Johnny shook his head with a sigh. "Don't pull a stunt like that when you're in town or people gonna fuck you up worse."

"I'm dead," the boy said. "How can I get worse?"

Johnny scoffed. "You're dead, but you ain't *dead*. Trust me, you don't wanna find out the difference. Now go on, scramble over to ya Maw's house. She'll be expecting you for breakfast."

The boy climbed up the pile of dirt and trudged away. Johnny sat down on the edge of the grave, swinging his legs back and forth as he took a drag off his cigarette. Fucking kids with their zombie movies. Necromancers got no respect these days.

———

WHEN JOHNNY'S PHONE RANG ON THURSDAY MORNING, HE didn't answer. He was tired. Too tired to deal with the annoying little shit he'd taken on as his apprentice Necromancer.

The phone chirped from the nightstand. He silenced it.

It rang a third time. Johnny huffed and shook his head. He probably hadn't taught the kid enough to cause too much trouble if he fired him now.

Johnny flipped his phone open and asked, "What now?"

"S-sorry to bother you, Mr. Nash, but there's a lady here to see you."

Johnny sighed. "I don't have any clients today, Eric. And I'm not taking any."

"Yes sir, I told her that."

"And?"

"And she still won't leave. She said she's an old friend of yours and she can't go without seeing you."

Johnny furled his brows. He didn't have any friends, old or new. "What's 'er name?"

Eric mumbled to the lady for a few seconds, then said, "Trixie West."

Johnny dropped the phone.

He picked it up and said, "Tell her I'll be right there."

JOHNNY STOOD IN FRONT OF THE BATHROOM MIRROR TRYING TO force his mustache to stay down. His mind raced with questions. Why was she here today? What did she remember? Where had she been since he'd last seen her?

It did no good to speculate. He'd find out soon enough.

He threw his underwear in the corner and pulled out some almost-clean ones from the pile of clothes in front of the chester-drawers. Rifling through the pile he found a tank top and his best cutoff jeans. Johnny considered wearing them, but no, Trixie's visit was far too important for his Sunday clothes. He turned to the closet and pulled the broken chain, sending the light bulb above swinging light and shadows through tiny space. He reached into the far corner and withdrew his lone button up. Black, of course, in remembrance of the greatest man to ever live—Johnny Cash. He put it on over his faded black Levi's while he toyed with the idea of a bolo.

"Too fancy," he mumbled.

Johnny picked up the raggedy Stetson from the top shelf. His papaw left him that hat, but dust and moths had taken a liking to it and left it worse for wear. Shaking his head, he swapped his Stetson for his lucky Sunoco hat and headed outside.

He glanced at the tarp in the yard that covered his '83 Camaro. He'd give his left nut to be able to get that baby restored. But his nuts didn't seem to be worth much these days, so the old pickup would have to do.

Johnny climbed into his truck and headed toward town. His mind wandered back to the times when he had a handful of vehicles to get downtown. In the beginning, there was a surprising amount of money to be had in necromancy, if you knew where to look.

And Johnny did know where to look: Logan County, West Virginia. He'd lived there all his life and understood the way people thought. His mama always said people were people no matter where you went, but Johnny didn't bother going. He figured if people were the same everywhere, he might as well stay where he was.

Johnny flicked his cigarette out the window just as he passed the entrance to Midelburg. He'd had a fine house in the rich part of town, neighbors who feared him and left him alone, and a steady income from *Nash's Necromancy*.

It had been a curiosity in the community, and a bit of a joke, for the first few months. Johnny hung posters and went door-to-door offering his services; he was asked to leave countless funerals, though he was volunteering his amenities pro bono to get the word out. No matter what he did, no one seemed to take him seriously.

That is, until he had his first customer. She was a young widow, just a wisp of a girl, and she wanted to see her dead husband. Johnny eagerly called the dead man's spirit up for the girl, and she eagerly cussed the spirit until Johnny's nose was bleeding from the effort of containing the spirit and holding the girl back.

After the young woman told everyone she knew about getting her peace from *Nash's Necromancy,* Johnny couldn't walk down the street without someone asking him to call up a long-dead relative. He'd gone from scraps for dinner— when there was dinner—to country-fried steak as often as he wanted.

Then the lawsuits came. People were upset about Johnny disturbing the natural order of things. He'd found comfort in drink, in trying to turn his fortune through the crank slots at Betty's Place. The big money dried up, leaving Johnny to feast on spam and saltines.

HE CLIMBED DOWN FROM HIS TRUCK AND STOOD IN FRONT OF THE shop window. It was a great location—center of town, right on the corner—and the owner was kind enough to let him use a booth for business so long as he bought a cup of coffee. Expensive shit, café o'lay or some dumb name, but it was worth it to keep a little money in his pocket.

Trixie stood in Hot Cup with her back to him, but even now he could feel butterflies tumbling in his belly at the sight of her. He remembered the first time he'd seen her on the playground when they were in the third grade. She was the prettiest thing he'd ever laid eyes on. Granted, he was only nine and his eyes hadn't seen much, but he knew what he knew—and what he knew was he was in love with Trixie West.

That day on the playground he'd decided to find a way to impress her and he knew exactly what to do: he was gonna show her how far he could spit. She was not impressed. Johnny was sure she would've been, if only the wind hadn't caught his loogie and blew it right into her hair.

He went through all the best tactics in the next few years, but no matter what he did, she seemed immune to his charms. He tried making her mud pies, showing her his new frog, bringing her flowers from Mrs. Pomeroy's front yard, and making her a friendship bracelet with a little cross charm. She would smile and thank him, all sweetness and civility, but nothing more.

The day came when Johnny couldn't take it anymore. He was going to tell her straight out that he loved her. He went to her mom's trailer and knocked. Mrs. West called Trixie for him. When she waddled toward the door, Johnny felt his jaw drop. He knew she hadn't been at school for awhile, and now he could see why. She couldn't hide that baby if she wanted to.

"I was worried since I ain't seen ya for a bit," he said. "And I wanted you to know that I missed you. Cause you know, I love you."

"You're sweet," she said, but her smile was sad. "You always were, Johnny Nash. I should've picked you."

EVEN IN JOHNNY'S MEMORY, THE DOOR CLOSING IN HIS FACE WAS painful. It was the end of the future he had envisioned with Trixie, though the love he carried for her never stopped. When he opened the door to the coffee shop, he felt like that little boy on the playground, seeing her for the first time.

"Hey Trixie," he said, pulling the hat from his head.

She smiled, sending butterflies through him. "Hiya Johnny. You look good."

"You too," he said. He ran his hand over his own hair and said, "I like your hair like that."

She dipped her head in thanks before saying, "I was hoping to talk to you privately. About business."

Johnny looked around. Eric the apprentice was staring at the interaction, incapable of disguising his interest in the conversation. Johnny hooked his thumb over his shoulder and said, "Beat it, kid."

Eric scurried from their regular booth and Johnny motioned for Trixie to take his place. He pressed his lips together, trying to smile, but trying not to look like he was trying to smile. Johnny opened his mouth to her to speak, but the words didn't feel right. He'd been reading people for years with his business, learning from the tics each displayed, and he could easily see she was nervous. Better to wait for her to explain than say something stupid.

He ordered them each a cup of coffee (eight damn dollars!). She seemed grateful for something to fill her hands. When she set the cup down, Johnny knew his cue to get down to business.

"What brings you in today, Miss West?"

She smiled. "You're not going to get formal on me, are you? We've known each other since we were kids."

Johnny nodded. "But you're here on business."

She cringed. Johnny knew then she didn't like being there, didn't like what he did. She was there because she was desperate.

"Who died?" he asked.

She watched her coffee, her lips slightly parted. Johnny had seen it many times. She'd made it that far, but wasn't sure if she should continue. But he knew she would. People were people.

"My daughter, Josie."

She looked up at him then, her eyes asking what she couldn't.

"You want to talk to her? No problem."

Trixie shook her head. Softly she said, "

Trixie placed her hand on his, her smile broadening. "That's great, Johnny. Real sweet of ya. But I was hopin' you could bring her back. Something…permanent."

Johnny inhaled sharply. The room felt tight around him.

"Trixie, I can't—" he said, pulling his hand away.

"Now don't you lie to me, Johnny P. Nash," she interrupted, all softness gone. "My cousin Rachel said you brought back her friend Bobbi Jean's baby when he died twelve years ago. I know you can do it."

Johnny swallowed. "Did she tell you what happened to the boy? To his mother?"

Trixie shook her head.

"Hell, your cousin might not've heard. I kept it pretty quiet."

"Heard what?"

"He was okay at first, or at least we thought he was. I kept tabs on him, just to make sure, you know?"

"Then what's the problem?"

Johnny's face scrunched up and he thought about not telling her, but she nodded her head for him to continue. "Bobbi Jean went in to feed him one day. She didn't need to, an' I told her that. Dead things don't eat. But she tried anyway. I guess the little bastard was done suckin' milk out of her tit and decided to try bitin' through it instead."

"Holy shit, Johnny."

He nodded. "Fucker wouldn't let go. She was trying so hard not to hurt him that she didn't pay attention to what he was doin' to her. Ate her brains right out. And it was my fault."

"You don't know that for sure."

"Yes, I do." Johnny bit his lip, trying to decide if he should tell her the thing he'd kept secret for so many years. After a moment, he took a deep breath and said, "He wasn't the first."

"What are you talking about?"

"I brought back another kid, a few years before that boy. Same thing."

Trixie couldn't stop the tears. Johnny had been her only chance.

"I can let you talk to her," he said. "I can even let her come back for a few days, but I can't make it last any longer than that or things get wonky inside them. I can't let her do that to you."

"She's the only good thing I ever had, Johnny."

"Come on, that can't be true," he said, moving his hand across the table toward hers.

"You don't fucking get it!" she screamed, pulling away her hand and slinging the coffee cup on the floor. "I have nothing. NOTHING. She was the only one I ever loved."

Johnny stood over her, his hand withdrawn, his heart aching for her. He understood.

———

Trixie spent the night.

Johnny wasn't surprised. She always did when she came looking for him. She never wanted to be alone after he told her he wouldn't bring her daughter back.

It had shocked him the first time. He'd looked on her body with reverence, a worshiper before his god. Now, he still loved her, enjoyed the nights he spent with her, but it was more a holiday than a holy day.

Johnny watched her as she dressed. She was always shy the morning after. But of course she was. For her, this was the first time it had happened. She didn't have the memory to ease her nerves.

"I guess I should go," she said. "Unless—"

"Unless I changed my mind?"

She nodded, shrugged. She walked toward him, steeling herself to say the words she always said. "You could do this thing for me, and I could do some things for you. A body for a body."

He'd considered it, the first time. But now there was no hesitation when he shook his head.

"I can't, Trixie."

She nodded. She was on the verge of tears, unable to speak. Johnny knew she would start crying if he didn't interrupt it now, so he did.

"There was another, Trix. One more person I didn't tell you about."

Her eyes found his, wide and excited, her hope igniting in her chest. "Did they, I mean, was it the same?"

Johnny shook his head. "Worse."

"Oh, Johnny, how could it be worse?"

He sighed. "When I heard you died, it broke me, Trix. I mean, I always loved you. Even when we were kids. Even when you didn't bother looking my way. So when I read your obituary, I had to do something. I wrote to the *American Institute of Necromantic Arts*, got them to agree to let me do a course by mail. It was hard, but I was motivated. Got my certification real quick, Trix, real quick for you.

"We talked first, your spirit and me. But it wasn't enough, when I knew I could do more. So I brought you back. You were my first. I didn't know what I was doing, so I didn't bind you well enough. I didn't know how to keep your needs in check. You went back to your little girl and ate her brains out."

Tears were rolling down her face. "This isn't funny Johnny P. Nash. You stop it right now."

"I covered it up for you. Car accident. I put you down to rest, until I thought I was ready to try again. So I raised you from the dead a second time. It was better. You were under control. You started making a life for yourself. Then your memories started to surface about your girl, and you ended up coming to me. It was part of the controls I'd put in when I brought you back the second time."

"This is cruel, Johnny. I never thought you'd be this cruel."

He stood and crossed the room. He picked up a plain box sitting on his mantle. Dipping his index finger in the box, he began to trace shimmery black circles across his bare chest.

"I've tried so many times, Trix. Everything I know to do, I've done. But I keep trying. Monday night, like clockwork, I raise you up. By Friday—Thursday this time, so maybe things are changing—the memories are back, well, at least partially; you know she's dead, but you don't remember doin' it. So I put you back in the grave and raise you again the next week."

Trixie was inching toward the door. Johnny flicked his wrist and she stopped, unable to move. He turned his hand, and as he did Trixie's body rotated toward him.

"I can't bring her back, Trixie. Necromancy has rules. If one of the dead destroys a person, they can't live again."

Trixie's whole body was trembling. "You're sayin' my Josie is gone for good? And it's all because you couldn't let go of a schoolboy crush?"

Johnny pressed his lips together. He crossed the room and smeared a shimmering black thumb across her cheek.

"I love you, Trixie. I always have. I'm gonna help you sleep now, and you're gonna forget all about this. We'll try again to get rid of those pesky memories."

"Don't you dare," she spat. "If you take away the last I have of my little girl, I'll never forgive you."

Johnny sighed and said, "I'll see you soon, babe."

"You'd better hope you never see me again, Johnny. Because I swear to you, I will find a way to kill you."

Johnny smiled. She always said that, every time. People are always people.

———

JOHNNY P. NASH WAS WAIST DEEP IN GRAVE DIRT FOR THE THIRD time that week. He laid out his tools and began his work. He didn't need to check the name on the headstone this time; it was there inside him, written on his heart.

HEAVENLY BODIES

CHAPTER 1
DURGLEBURGLESTAHP

I t's your first vacation together and you want to make it special. You buy a cruise to the Heavenly Body because you've heard that she is both beautiful and accommodating to tourists. You wonder how they know it's a *she*, but then the ship crests Alpha Scorpii and you can see past the red supergiant, where the Body bathes in its glow.

She is spectacular. Glowing. Luminescent. Regardless of the genitalia unseeable from this angle, she is undeniably feminine. Now that you've seen her aura with your own six eyes, you wonder how you ever questioned that she is a *she*. There's no way you will ever see her as anything else.

You look at Clarina staring awestruck at the Body, and you feel a twinge in your heart for this strange bipedal humanoid. You've never seen her look at anything with as much open-mouthed wonder and part of you is jealous, just a tiny bit, of the admiration she's giving your vacation destination.

But mostly you're full of your own awestruck wonder as you take in Clarina. You've never loved a woman before. And that's what this is, you think. Maybe it's time. Your Brood-mother certainly thinks so and has been quite verbal about it, especially since all twelve-thousand and eight of your siblings started molting, leaving you and Griedlebouise as the only remaining children of the Great Broodmother Bringladersen who haven't found a mate. And stars above, no one wants to be like Griedlebouise.

You hear someone behind you ask, "She's amazing, isn't she?"

And you nod, say yes, though you know you're talking about different things because your eyes haven't left Clarina.

CHAPTER 2
CLARINA

Everyone warned you not to date a Habberblüterbrood, but did you listen? No. Of course not. Because you know best. And maybe Durgleburglestahp is different from the rest of the broodlings. Maybe Durg won't come on super strong and super fast and super...molty? Is that a word? Molty? You don't think so, but there's no other way to explain it.

So you go on a date with Durg and it's fine. They treat you well, opening airlocks for you, helping you adjust to the low gravity of the restaurant, and even sampling your food to make sure it was consumable for your species. When it wasn't, they sent it back for you and requested something else, remaining firm but not fussy. It impressed you how they didn't splash on the waiter even though you could see they were boiling, upset that you'd been brought a hamblargher instead of a hamburger, the difference between them being deadly.

After that one nearly perfect date, it was easy to say yes to a cruise to the Heavenly Body. You were a little unsure, afraid that this might be typical brood behavior, but you had made your intentions to Durg clear on the first date: your career comes first. They know that you're not in this for love, and you're certainly not ready to be a broodmother.

Besides, how could anyone pass up a chance to explore the Body? An alien so vast that you can land on her, explore her for days, weeks even, and never see the same place twice? Except the landing zone, you think, because you'd have to see that twice. But you digress.

Now as you stare out at her, feeling the glorious weight of anxiety piling on you as you realize how tiny you are in the great expanse of the universe, you can't help but also feel the weight of Durg's gaze on you. It feels heavier than the existential crisis forming in your ape-brain, and you suddenly realize you've made a terrible mistake.

CHAPTER 3
DURGLEBURGLESTAHP

You exit the starcruiser near the navel. It's warm here, warmer than you prefer, and you know you'll have to shed a layer of skin to find any comfort. You aren't sure that Clarina is ready for that; yeah, sure, you've been dating for a long time now, more than double any of your past relationships, but shedding in front of someone is a big deal and even though *you're* ready, you want to make sure she is, too.

So instead you find the little *blütes'* room and squeeze into a stall that was definitely made with smaller lifeforms in mind. Your layer sloughs off but you can't get it to flush and there's no plunger. You hear someone outside tapping their toes, waiting for a stall, so you linger inside as quietly as possible and hope another stall opens up soon so you can leave without anyone seeing what you've done.

When you finally make it back to Clarina, she's talking to another humanoid and you feel that twinge of jealousy inside again, but you force a smile anyway. Your smile turns genuine when she waves you over and places a hat on your head—a hat she picked out for you in the ship's gift shop. The human-man-thing, Chad, gives his farewell and joins his companion who has also just left the restrooms. When you see them laughing together, you *know* it's about your shedding. You spend the rest of the afternoon sulking and avoiding the group.

You mope through dinner, even though you're at a lovely breast-side bar and grille that claims to serve the best Warmusgarv in the galaxy. Clarina wants to walk through the garden and menagerie after, but you can't escape your mood. You realize this would be a great place to give her the gift you got her in secret, but when Chad and his companion ask to join you, you drop back into melancholy and the box weighs heavy in your skin flap, unopened.

CHAPTER 4
CLARINA

Durg has been THE WORST on this trip and you know it won't get better anytime soon. They won't talk about whatever is bothering them, instead preferring to sulk at whichever accommodation you're staying at for the night. This has for sure not been a good second date and part of you thinks you should do a better job vetting those you go out with, but another part of you is like, "Free trip!"

Thank god you met Chad and Blain right after landing or you'd be having a miserable time. With Durg back at the resort, you're out skiing the middle neck (less head-winds from this one than the other two) with the other humans. You know that this will bother Durg; in fact, you're counting on it. This trip has made it clear that your time with Durg will be short. Your only goal now is to make it through the rest of the week without breaking their bulbous hearts.

"What's up with your friend," Chad asks as you stop at the bottom of the neck to wait for Blain. He's not a great skier, but he tells funny stories, so you don't mind waiting.

You shrug, unsure what to say. "They've been weird since we got here," you say. "I thought I was imagining it at first, but it's gotten worse every day."

"If you need to bail, you can stay with us," Chad says.

You're grateful, and you say so, but you know Durg would be upset and you don't want to hurt them, especially not in front of the whole tour group.

At dinner you try to pull Durg out of their funk. You order a fizzy gurgleslurp for two and laugh as it tickles your throat. It makes Durg cough, souring their mood again. They barely touch their food and weird you out by keeping one tentacle in their skin flap through the whole meal.

Back in the room, you suggest they sleep on the couch.

CHAPTER 5
DURGLEBURGLESTAHP

You're watching Clarina slide down the ear canal. She's already done it four or five times, but she laughs every time. You smile along with her, but you can't bring yourself to do more. You were really put off when she asked you to sleep on the couch last night, especially after you were having such a perfect evening up until then.

But your Broodmother always said humanoids were strange creatures, prone to drama, and maybe that was just a taste of it.

Doesn't matter though. Tonight you'll board the boat to sail down the back and you'll arrive at the tentacle-hip at dawn. Every review you've read says this is the most romantic part of each trip. You're going to get up early and get breakfast—for Clarina that's usually just the bitter drink she likes—put out fluberbuds with red petals and snow-white wings, and wake her up while down on three knees, holding her gift aloft. You've read about the tradition in human stories and you want to do things right for Clarina.

You don't think she'll be surprised though. At this point, you've been together so long you're surprised she hasn't demanded your life-promise already. She's hinted at it, sure, especially on this trip, but you weren't ready before. You are now. She's put in the time and she deserves this, but also, you love her.

CHAPTER 6
CLARINA

"**N**o."

CHAPTER 7
DURGLEBURGLESTAHP

You're standing on the stern, watching the Heavenly Body disappear behind Alpha Scorpii. She's so beautiful it hurts to say goodbye to her. Just before the last of her falls behind the supergiant, she turns her head and looks directly at you. For a second, you think she winked one of her massive moon-sized eyes. The thought makes you smile.

Heading to the bar you see your ex, Clarina. She's with the other humans and you can tell she's sad, even though she laughs louder than you've ever heard her. The breakup was hard on her, but it's been ages now and you hope eventually she'll move on. You don't stick around; alas, the poor thing is fragile, and you don't want to give her false hope that you have any lingering feelings.

You spot Arkevine at a booth in the corner and make your way to her. She looks radiant tonight, wearing a carapace that glitters topaz and peridot, and you're surprised you haven't seen it before since you've been together so long. As you reach the table, you let a tentacle slide over the box in your skin flap and say, "I have a gift for you, darling."

PATRIOTS VS. ALIENS IN AREA 51

Originally published in *Storming Area 51* by Black Hare Press

CHAPTER 1

PATRIOTS VS. ALIENS IN AREA 51

've been waitin' nineteen years for a chance to get them sons a'bitches, ever since they took my wife and impregnated her. Now I don't know what them aliens look like, or how many arms they got or nothin'. My wife don't remember much about that weekend. But she had a boy, looks human, and acts human, but I know he's theirs just as sure as I know the workday is long. I got snipped at forty, she had him after, and it's surely because of them little green men.

I saw the Area 51 raid on Facebook while I was checking out a local yard sale group. Some of 'em were jokin' about rescuing aliens and havin' new space-pets, but I knew better. Those things aren't fit to be around us normal folks. I see it everyday with my wife's spawn, *Brandon*. Oh, he tries to fit in and he pretends to be normal, but I know he ain't. And he knows I know. But I digress.

Soon as I saw the ad, I knew what I needed to do. I called Steve, Dale, and Rick—my boys from the Legion, sans Darren (that fool would get us all killed). We made plans to head to Charleston for a gun show a couple weeks later. Until then, we'd meet in my garage, throw back a few cold ones, and make a plan.

The plan didn't come together like I thought it would, but

it didn't dampen our spirits. We knew we were in the right, and the good Lord would back us against those alien mother-fuckers. I talked to Pastor Mac about it and he agreed there was no better cause than to take up arms against them that would enter our country illegally. Now that I think about it, seems he might've been talkin' about Mexicans. As my President says, they ain't sending their best, but if they can point a gun at the real aliens, I say we let 'em stay.

Anyways, after stocking up at the gun show and borrowing my cousin's winnebago, we were ready to meet our brethren in Nevada. Now I'd seen some mock-ups on the internet, but most of the plans seemed amateur at best. Still, I didn't know what their Nar-you-tow runners were and thought maybe they had some secret weapons, so I had hope.

I kissed Shirley full on the lips while she flipped my eggs —somethin' I hadn't done for years. The excitement of what was about to happen had my stomach doin' cartwheels and I almost couldn't eat the three eggs, sausage, bacon, fried pota-toes, and toast that she made me. But I did. Who knows when we may get a chance to eat again? As I passed through the livin' room, I saw Brandon passed out on the couch with a bag of funyuns on his chest and an empty jar of pickles on the floor beside tipped over empty cans of Budweiser.

"Damn aliens," I muttered. "Won't get a job like the rest of us red-blooded Americans, can't pass a damn drug test, and expect my tax dollars to support their sorry asses. Well, I tell you what, Trump won't have it and neither will I."

I slung my duffel bag over my shoulder, grabbed my Earnhardt hat, and marched my happy ass out to the garage with renewed vigor. Steve was there at a quarter to eight and we compared weapons, trying to determine which would be best for sniping, hauling over the terrain from gate to facility, and those for close combat. In the end, we decided to take 'em all. Can't be too careful.

While we were loadin' the camper, Dale and Rick showed

up and added their gear to the mix. We climbed in and were just about to pull out when a white '78 Trans Am jerked to a stop in front of us. The bird painted across the front seemed to scream at me as I stared, stunned, at the figure who approached. Shoulder-length hair the color of mud was tied back with a red, white, and blue bandana. He wore camo cargo shorts and a black shirt with the sleeves cut off, guns over each pale shoulder.

In short, he looked badass.

"What's he doin' here?" Rick asked. "Thought we weren't tellin' him about the raid."

Dale winced. "It might've slipped out."

Now Darren is what I call "batshit." So it didn't bode well when he climbed up in the winnie and gave a snuff-stained grin. He said, "You weren't leavin' without me, were ya?"

"Course not," I lied. "Figured you was just runnin' late and we wanted to be ready to go."

Darren tossed his bag and weapons on the floor and slumped back against a seat. "Good. I'd've been mighty red if you'd gone on without me."

Without another word, I put 'er in drive and we headed out for our mission.

———

WE MADE IT TO MOUNT STERLING, KENTUCKY BEFORE WE HAD to stop. Darren's morning constitutional left us gasping for air and rolling down the windows wasn't enough. Fifteen minutes parked with the windows down and doors open, plus Steve's splurge on an aerosol freshener, let us get back on the road.

"You can't be doin' that the whole trip," Rick said. He don't like Darren all that much, never has, and his patience was already wearin' thin.

Darren just stared back with a shit-eatin' grin as he

squirted canned cheese into his mouth. I smelled disaster for those two idgets unless I could keep 'em apart, so I called on Steve, my best friend and the only decent man among us, to take the wheel. I moved Rick up front beside him and spent my time watching Dale whittle and listening to Darren fart.

We stopped for dinner in St. Louis. The cornbread muffins were good, the barbecue was fine, but it was the busty gal behind the counter that made the little joint worth rememberin'. Rick took a likin' to her, too, and when she went on break he gave her a tour of the winnebago. We stayed inside and finished our drinks, even having a round of apple pie while we gave him time to finish his business. He's been mighty lonely since Armelia died, and there ain't one of us who would blame him for wantin' a little comfort.

The girl returned twenty minutes later, smoothing her hair and uniform like we didn't all know what happened. When we got back to the winnie, Rick wasn't there. The bed was mussed and air smelled sweaty, so we rolled down the windows for the second time while we waited.

"Prolly in the pisser," Dale said as he kicked off his boots. He pointed across the parking lot to the gas station.

"Makes sense," I agreed. Steve turned the ole girl toward the station.

A *thwap-thwap* under the wheels made us all jump. There weren't no speed bumps in this lot. Steve pulled up a bit farther and we checked the mirrors. A flanneled lump lay on the ground behind us.

The cops came and took statements from the lot of us. We didn't know why he'd been under there. The last one to see him alive was the waitress. I went in with the cop to point her out, but she wasn't there. They talked to the manager, who acted like he had no idea who I was talkin' about.

"The one with the red curls and the big tits," I said. It was the only thing I remembered.

"We don't have any redheads on staff," the manager said.

I floundered for words until Steve stepped up beside me and put his hand on my shoulder. He said, "I don't know who you're coverin' for, but we know what we saw."

The cops seemed to take his words as gospel, turning their attention from us to the manager. One of the officers waved us away and said he'd call us when they figured out what happened. Back in the winnie it was a somber affair. Rick had been one of our disenfranchised brothers for years. The thought of leaving him behind was heavy.

"Let's turn back," Dale said, his voice seeming to rip as it came from his lips.

Steve shook his head. "That's not what Rick would want."

I looked at him, surprised by his words. Steve is mild-mannered on his most rebellious days. He sings in the choir with his wife every Sunday, he volunteers to take meals to shut-ins, he plays Santa for the Christmas toy drive. He also happens to be a former Special Ops and did two tours in Kuwait in the early nineties. But he doesn't talk about what happened over there. Instead he talks about his daughter, the teacher, or his son studying up at WVU. So even knowing what I knew about Steve, I never expected him to want to press on.

That's probably why we did. Steve's words were steel, resolve in our backbones, and we kept going.

We were somewhere in Colorado, about twelve hours from the alien daycare, when we lost Dale. The park ranger said he was in the wrong place at the wrong time, a mountain lion dragged him under the bus, and we were lucky he was the only victim.

'Course I knew he was fulla malarkey. Losing Rick was bad, real bad, but losing Dale the same way was downright scary. I knew it had to be Darren—he's never been quite right anyway. And in some sick way I understood why he killed Rick. It had been a constant war between 'em. But Dale was his friend; his only friend, if I'm bein' honest.

I tried to talk to Steve about it the next time we stopped for gas, but Darren was always close. Steve shook his head to keep me from sayin' more, but I knew he understood what I was gettin' at.

"We gotta keep movin'," he said. "We'll be there soon enough and can sort this whole mess out."

He was right, but I didn't like it. There was too much space between us and there, too much time for another strike. But there was nothin' else to do but keep drivin'.

————

WE REACHED A51 IN THE EVENIN' WHEN ALL THE OTHER campers and trucks and motorcycles were parkin'. As we pulled in by a lifted F150, I breathed a sigh of relief. These were my people, and their presence made me feel safe. Then a Tesla pulled in beside us and that safety dwindled a bit.

There were plenty of people who looked serious standin' around with guns and knives strapped to 'em, but there were also a bunch of teeny-boppers in convertibles drinkin' craft beer and smokin' doobies. I shook my head. My wife's alien freeloader would be right at home here.

When the time came, we were all in it together. The rednecks with the hipsters, the tech-nerds and the UFC wannabes, the bikers and the business men. Turns out everyone wanted to see what the government was keepin' secret. It's the most united I've seen our great country in a long time.

Nobody really knew what we were doin'. Lotta people got shot. Those runners I'd read about had been a joke about some cartoon. Damn millennials. Still, me, Steve, and Darren got in. Luck, I guess, 'cause it sure wasn't because of our good planning.

Inside was a maze of chaos. I opened a door only to immediately close it when I saw—well, I don't rightly know what it was, but I knew I didn't want to see it again. A line of spidery-things the size of my hound crawled past and no one bothered stoppin' them. I saw people in lab coats leading chains attached to slendermen, black oozes that left a trail of glitter in their wake, and a short gray thing with a bulbous head that carried a minia-ture version of itself as it searched through the crowd for an exit.

As I stood there staring at everything and everyone, I didn't even bother to pull out one of my guns. It was too much and I didn't know where to start shootin'. I stepped back into an empty corridor and watched while a warm, wet spot formed on the front of my pants.

Then I saw the weirdest thing of all: the top of Steve's head flipped back and revealed a huge mouth with the biggest teeth I've ever seen. He pulled Darren to him and took a massive bite. Blood and meat fell all around him, but he didn't seem to notice. He flipped his head back over and wiped his mouth. He looked up and our eyes met.

I fell down then. Guess my body was shakin' too hard for my legs to hold me up. Steve pushed his way toward me through the press of bodies. I was callin' down fire from Heaven with every step he took, but he kept gettin' closer. When he reached me, he slid down the wall beside me until he was sittin' on the floor.

"Sorry you had to see that," he mumbled, somehow managing to look sheepish.

"You ate Darren."

He nodded. "Dale and Rick, too. I didn't mean to. I've been keepin' myself in check all these years and didn't think it would bother me. But the closer we got to this place, the stronger my hunger became."

"You gonna eat me, too?"

"I'll try not to. Already did you a disservice once."

"What are you talkin' about?" I ask.

He looked at me with a pained expression. "Knockin' up your wife."

"Shit," I mutter. "So Brandon really is an alien? I just thought Shirley cheated on me."

"I guess it's both. She cheated, and he's an alien."

We sat there in silence for a few minutes and for that time, it felt like we were in my man cave watchin' NASCAR with nary a care in the world.

Finally I said, "Well, I guess I should be gettin' back. You gonna stick around for awhile?"

Steve nodded. "Yeah. Prolly eat those assholes with the Prius."

I chuckled, "They kinda deserve it."

"It was good knowin' you, Earl," he said, shakin' my hand. "You've been the best friend I've had in the last three hundred years."

"Will I ever see you again?" I ask, hopin' and fearin' his answer.

"Don't reckon you will. Your world won't last long after this mess and I've got places to be."

"Should I give your wife a message?"

"Nah, she'll be along shortly with the kids. But thanks." We stare at each other again before I see Steve's head start to tip back. He said, "Get goin' before I eat ya."

And I did. Ran straight out the building, past the fights ragin' on and the bullets zippin' by. I got in the winnebago and locked the doors, leaned back in my seat, and spent the rest of the night watching the spaceships dartin' overhead as they made their way home.

At first light, I did the same.

GRANDMA ASSASSINS IN OUTER SPACE

Originally published in *Adventure Awaits vol 3* by Breaking Rules Europe

CHAPTER 1
GRANDMA ASSASSINS IN OUTER SPACE

When we colonized the moon in 2053, all the remaining wonder left the world. At least, that's what my grandma says. She was just a girl then, nine or ten, but she seems to remember it like it was yesterday.

"The moon, Vini," she says, staring up at the night sky. "It used to be a thing of beauty and mystery! Now, it's just another country."

She has said these words to me a hundred times—twice this week—and I have my response ready for her, like reading from a script. "What was it like, Nunu?"

"Oh, sweet girl, it was glorious. You could only see it at night, mind you, but it glowed bright back then, without those ridiculous lights that cover it now."

"You can see it all the time now. Isn't that better?"

She huffed, like always. "What good does that do us, when we're still down here?"

She doesn't know how much it hurts to hear those words. I know she wouldn't say them if she did. I've told her before about the mission, about how I'm leaving tonight to fly to the dark side of the moon before I head off for the colony on Titan. I've even tearfully told her about how I probably won't see her again, about how I'm saying goodbye to everything and everyone and venturing off into the unknown, in the hopes of creating a future for the generations who come after me.

But she doesn't remember. Maybe it's better that way.

"You cold, Nunu?" I ask, watching goose pimples parade up the paper-thin flesh of her arms. "Want a blanket?"

"Pah," she says, as if it is an answer.

For her, I suppose it is. I've heard it so many times growing up, I know it means: *"Leave me alone and stop worrying, you little shit."* Or perhaps, *"I'm old, not incapable, you little shit."* Either way, "you little shit" is always implied.

I get her a blanket anyway, as well as her favorite brittle, and we sit cuddled up on her patio for another hour, watching the moon in silence. It might be too bright for her, but for me it shines with possibility.

When curfew nears in her retirement community—old hag confinement village, she calls it—I'm hesitant to go. I must, of course, and my brain knows that, but my heart aches at the thought. My grandmother dedicated her forties and fifties to raising a brat no one wanted. She spent her sixties and seventies cheering that same brat on as she made something of herself, a feat only achieved by the desire to make Nunu proud.

She kept my head on straight, showed me how to be a contributing member to the future of society, and saw through my shit when I tried to give it. I love her more than anyone else in the universe, and I'm leaving her to spend her final days in this place, alone.

Without thinking, I say, "Come on, Nunu. We're going on a trip."

She squints out from under what little eyebrows she has left. "Where are we going, Vin?"

"I'm breaking you out of here."

A smile creeps across her face, slow and steady and magnificent, before she says, "It's about damn time."

———

Nunu used to tell me stories about space. I don't know where she heard them, or if she made them up, but they were glorious. There was always a sassy lady pilot who bucked the system, or a foxy assassin with a heart of gold, or, in my favorite one, a ragtag group of space-pirates looking for the Davy Jones of the stars. Whatever the story, she made sure I could see myself in one of the characters, that I knew I could do anything. She's the reason I joined the planetary exploration unit.

And now, as I smuggle my eighty year old grandmother aboard a ship headed to the moon, she's likely the reason I'll be expelled from the P.E.U.

We cross through the first barrier with a flash of my smile —the guard has seen me every day for the last eight months and I'm pretty sure has a crush on me, without picking up on the fact that he is as far from my type as you can get. The second barrier checks my badge and rummages through my trunk for anything dangerous, but they don't seem to register the elderly woman in my passenger seat.

To say this surprises me would be an understatement. Nunu always says that old people become more like furniture as they age: invisible unless you run into it. This is the first time I've witnessed it. I don't know what I expected to happen when we rolled up to a government-run scientific facility with a white-haired sass machine who definitely was not on the guest list, but it wasn't this.

But this is exactly what she said would happen.

I tried to get her to hide in my duffel bag and she gave me a death glare. I suggested she lie on the backseat with a blanket over her and she "Pah'd" at me again. "I'll ride up front with you, Vini," she'd said.

"They won't let you pass," I'd tried to rebut.

"No one will stop us, dear. Trust your Nunu."

Since there wasn't another choice, I did what she said. Though I assumed they would end up calling my piece-o'-shit dad to come and take her back to the old folks' home when we tried to go through the first barrier, I drove on like she was exactly where she was supposed to be, and somehow she became just another piece of my luggage.

Now though, we're out of the car and in line at the final checkpoint that allows us into the facility. I have no idea how I'm going to get her past the last guard, and I only have as long as it takes them to check in the half a dozen people in front of us to figure it out.

My mind is drawing a blank as the line dwindles. I lean over and whisper, "I don't think we're going to make it, Nunu."

She pats my arm and says, "You need to have a little more faith in your grandma."

I grin, unable to help myself. Her confidence is ridiculous. I wish I could borrow a bit of it some time, since she's always been overflowing with it. Still, I've got no clue what to say to the guards, and whatever her plan is, she's keeping it to herself.

With two people left in front of us, Nunu takes hold of my left elbow and seems to dissolve into herself. Her perfect posture is now hunched, head bent, and she looks frail. My breath hitches in my throat. It's the first time I've looked at her and truly seen her eighty years, without her bravado backing her up. I don't like it.

"Present your wrist, please."

I catch eyes with the guard and step up, turning my wrist so he can scan in. It beeps an acceptance and I see the man's eyes widen ever so slightly as he sees my rank come up on his screen.

"Apologies, Major, I didn't recognize you."

"No reason you would, Guardian. I'm a civvy now."

A chuckle seems to rise in his throat but he cuts it off. "Yeah, the one leading the Titan mission."

I smile as brightly as I can manage through my anxiety, but the young man hasn't seemed to notice my grandmother clinging to my arm. "Put in your time, Specialist. There will be plenty of opportunities for you once you're my age."

"Because of you, Major," he says, drawing his hand up in salute. "Thank you for your service."

I return the gesture and step past him, buoyed by the man's sincerity, and also by the fact that my grandma is some sort of sneaky ninja woman who can go wherever the hell she wants without anyone noticing her. She'd make a damn fine spy, were she so inclined.

Though I want to stop and celebrate with her, I don't, afraid to draw attention to her after such luck. Instead, we march through the facility like we own the place; with my pride nearly swallowing me whole and her constant unearned confidence, we pass a dozen more guards on walk-about as we head down the main corridor without batting an eye. We're unstoppable.

———

THE SHIP TAKING US TO THE MOON IS A PASSENGER SHIP. Somehow this surprises my grandmother, and as she walks circles around my small room, she continuously talks about the old combustion rockets that were used back in the old days.

"Nunu," I say, interrupting her third time telling me about how the payload fairing separates prior to orbital insertion, which is something she knows nothing about. "We haven't used those types of rockets for forty years."

She stops pacing and levels a "how dare you" look at me. "You think I don't know that? You were born the same day the first QI rocket launched. I was so thrilled, I would have named you 'Unruh,' after the radiation converted to thrust, if only your parents had been cool with it."

I smile as she starts her pacing again. Now that she's said it, I remember her calling me *little Unruh* when I was a kid. I didn't understand it then, so I would insist on my full name, Alvinia. Now that I've heard why she called me that, I'd kill to have her use it again.

A bell chimes overhead and the lights dim, coming back up with a red tint. A synthetic AI voice radiates from the speaker above the door, saying, *"Good evening, guests. This is your Captain speaking. Welcome aboard the* Falcon 76, *the smart choice for all your space-faring needs. Please secure yourself for initial takeoff which will take effect in four minutes."*

My eyes dart to Nunu, and I can see we're thinking the same thing: *shit.*

Considering that I'm in a single occupant room, with single occupant securing facilities, but there are actually two of us, the thought is concise, but accurate. She scurries about the room in the hopes that there's an emergency harness somewhere, but I know better. These may be passenger rockets, but they're not designed for comfort, and certainly not made with the expectation of stowaways.

"Two minutes," the AI Captain says.

"Strap in," Nunu says, pressing her hand against my stomach and pushing me against the wall.

"No way," I say. "You strap in and I'll climb in the closet with my bag."

"Don't be a fool. We're both using the straps." I feel my lips move into a fish-like pucker as she continues, "We barely make one good-sized man if we smoosh together. Get in the harness, then I'll get in, and all is well."

I do as she says. I don't know if this is a good idea, but we don't have time to argue. As I secure the harness around us, I feel an itch in the back of my brain, begging to berate me for the genius idea of bringing an elderly runaway onto the ship. I don't scratch the itch, hoping ignoring my stupidity will somehow make it go away. As I fasten the last buckle around Nunu's chest and wrap my arms around her, I'm fairly confident my foolishness will persist, as both a feature and a flaw.

We listen to the countdown, and if Nunu is as certain of our pending demise as I am, she doesn't say so. In fact, with her back pressed against my stomach, I'm fairly sure I can feel her humming.

The seconds tick by in what feels like an eternity of waiting, until finally we hear the engine burst into life and the shake of the ship rattles our teeth. Dimly I wonder if Nunu's dentures will fall out and the crew will find us hanging here tomorrow, my arms wrapped around a tiny old lady with no teeth.

Instead, in a very short time later, far shorter than I imagined even with my knowledge and preparation by the P.E.U., the turbulence ceases and the calm voice of the Captain says, *"We are now outside Earth's atmosphere and making our way toward the Independent Nation of the Moon. Our expected arrival time is in twelve hours. Feel free to release your harness and walk about your cabin. As always,* Falcon 76 *and all of SpaceX appreciates your dedication to safety."*

Before I can unhook the harness, Nunu has already pressed the release and extricated herself from the safety equipment. She looks back at me, a broad grin on her face, and says, "Well, that certainly was anticlimactic."

———

THE MOON LANDING GOES MUCH THE SAME. ASIDE FROM SOME mild turbulence as the craft settles down, it's an amazingly smooth ride. We disembark into the moonbase and make our way to the observation deck. I need to check in soon, but there's no way I'm going to pass up the chance to see my grandmother's face as she looks out over the place she's spent her life looking up to.

We stand by the railing, looking through the clear dome at the craggy surface of the moon. Nunu doesn't say anything, but she grips my elbow with a force that says she's happy, she's overwhelmed, she's trying not to cry. I swallow against my own emotion boiling up inside. This has been a long time coming.

After the newness of the visual spectacle has passed, we head off through the base in search of breakfast. Though the station we're in now was initially established as a scientific base, it now sprawls across the moon, branching into new housing developments, entertainment plazas, shopping markets, and tourist traps that give you the "real moon experience." I'd like to believe Nunu and I are both smart enough to avoid such places, but when you can get Neil Armstrong's famous moon pancakes AND a photo beside a piece of the original lander for the low, low price of ninety-nine credits, it's a no brainer.

While we're in line for our picture, Nunu sidles in close beside me and whispers, "Do not turn your head,"—at which point I immediately turn my head and she swats at me—"but there is a man back there in a black jacket who has been eyeing us since the observation deck."

I sigh. She had me worried for a second. "It's probably just another person who came up on the *Falcon.* Maybe he followed us because he wasn't sure where to go."

She purses her lips. "I get a bad vibe from him."

"You get a bad vibe from the postman."

"And I was right, too. That man was caught stealing packages."

"There's also the possibility that he recognizes me," I say, trying to keep my voice even. I hate the way it sounds like bragging to say such a thing, but it is possible. My face has been all over the newsfeeds for weeks leading up to the Titan mission.

Now it's her turn to roll her eyes. "Oh, right, because you're so important now."

"That's not what I—"

"He's moving away. He must've caught me watching him," she whispers.

"I'm sure that's it."

"Pah," she growls, and I'm certain I hear, *Don't patronize me, you little shit.*

———

AFTER BREAKFAST, I GO TO CHECK INTO MISSION CONTROL. There's no way Nunu can get through security there, no matter how much she insists it's possible, so I hesitantly leave her inside a series of joined shops boasting to be the moon's largest outlet mall. I don't feel great about leaving her behind, but she assures me if anyone gives her trouble, she'll fake a heart attack and make a scene.

I kinda feel bad for anyone who might mess with her.

Check in is smooth. After we've all found our assigned areas and moved into our home for the next six months, I give a rousing speech to encourage the settlers. I harken back to the days when this same trip would've taken over three years. I speak of the names we all know—Neil Armstrong, Guion Bluford, Sally Ride, Mae Jemison, Ash Musk, Michael Yuen, Phạm Tuân—and then I read from the Titan's manifest the names the world will never forget. The assembly is full of excitement as I conclude, and I have to admit I'm pretty happy with myself as well.

We have two hours to tie up any loose ends before we ship off. For most people, it means a final call to their loved ones who stayed behind. For me, however, it means finishing what I put off before, what I dread to do: I have to say goodbye to my grandmother, for real this time.

As I head out of the mission area, I catch sight of a man lurking just outside the security perimeter. He's tall and brawny, with dark hair shaved to a stubble and eyes as black as the jacket he wears. Eyes that happen to be locked on me.

I offer a tentative smile that is not returned. I never saw the man Nunu was convinced was watching us, but I'm sure this can't be the same man. No, this is just some exploration enthusiast excitedly waiting for the launch. I will not subscribe to a paranoid story that says otherwise. Though really, the ideas would fit quite well with the adventure stories Nunu used to tell me.

I keep walking. If there's trouble to be had, I'm sure I'll find it. Accidentally, of course. But the guards will take care of any issues that arise. My priority right now has to be my last farewell.

As I make my way back to the mall, I'm struck with the skin-crawling feeling of someone watching me. I check my surroundings repeatedly, but nothing seems out of place. The man in the black jacket is gone, or has at least blended in enough to avoid my detection. Though I try to shake off the feeling, it persists while I walk through the shops, searching for a tiny old woman who can't be seen if she's behind a rack of clothes.

The mall is bigger than I realized, and my paranoia is growing stronger every minute. I go to the information desk and have them page Ms. Eloise Harbinger, but she never comes.

When my time is nearly up and I've mentally beat myself

up as much as humanly possible, I walk back to Titan head-quarters to prepare for departure. I am completely broken up about what I've done. I have selfishly brought an octoge-narian *to the freaking moon* without even the semblance of a plan, just because I felt guilty leaving her in her safe, comfort-able home. And now I've lost her in a giant lunar mall.

Cool. Coo-uhl. Cool, cool, cool.

I'm on the settlement ship walking toward my room, my heart is so downtrodden, my mind so distracted, I barely notice the black-jacketed man standing in the corridor in front of me, along with two other unsavory characters. By the time I do give them my attention, noting with a frown that they aren't supposed to be aboard the ship, I know it's too late.

WHEN I COME TO, IT'S THE SOUND OF THINGS THAT DRAWS MY attention back to the land of the living. Or rather, the absence of sound. The darkness around me is unnaturally quiet. Tomblike. Then I realize my eyes are still closed.

I open them only a sliver, but it's too much. The light is far too bright, the room around me awash in sterile white and stainless silver, and in the back of my mind I wonder if I have a concussion. But I open them a tinge more and realize I'm where I'm supposed to be, inside a cryo-bed, on my way to…

No, that's not right. Cryo-beds were supposed to be used if there was danger. Put ourselves to sleep and wait for rescue. I must've been dreaming before. Taking Nunu to the moon, getting chased by men in black jackets—none of that could've been real. I scrub a hand over my face, wiping away the ice crystals clinging to my lashes.

I press the release on my cryo-bed as a figure approaches above. A rescue worker, probably, from whatever danger we were in. I smile and blink at them before I fully register who's in front of me: a short woman, white hair shaved on the sides and spiked on top. Though wrinkles cross her forehead and cause her thin lips to sag, her hazel eyes are vibrant and full of life. My Nunu, standing in front of me in a long grey duster with massive daggers strapped to her belts, looks like a fucking badass.

She reaches a hand over to help me out of the cryo-bed and says, "Come with me if you want to live."

———

I FOLLOW HER TO THE DOOR, PAUSING WHEN SHE PUTS A HAND up. In films, this means I should be quiet. While following a tough-looking old lady out of a creepy science lab, the vibe is pretty much the same.

A moment later, she flips her hand around and motions me to follow. We jog down the hall, the squeak of her combat boots on the floor the only indication of our presence. At the end of the hall, she stops us again, peeks around the corner, then darts across and into the adjacent room.

We're immediately met with the business end of a ray gun, though I'm not sure what sort this one is. I suppose the type of ray doesn't really matter when it's pointed in your face.

"Thank fuck," the woman holding it says as she lowers it to her side.

Without the thought of imminent death at her hands, I take a moment to get a good look at her. Her skin is dark, natural black and gray curls cropped short. Her face is fuller than my grandma's, less wrinkled, but I think she's nearly the same age. She's dressed similarly to Nunu, though her forest green jacket isn't as long and she only has the one knife tucked into her tall boot instead of two at her belt. She's rounder than my grandma, and a little taller; when she was young, I would almost guarantee people referred to her as voluptuous.

"Vini, I'd like to introduce you to the one and only Josephine Baker," Nunu says as Ms. Baker hooks an arm around my grandma's waist and pulls her close. She presses a kiss against Nunu's temple and my grandmother practically melts. She turns back to me a second later and adds, "My wife."

I press a hand against my chest as surprise roils through me. "You're gay?"

Nunu smirks. "Did you think you were the only one?"

"What? No, of course not. It's just, you never said..."

"And you never asked."

"But you could've told me."

She shrugs. "Never seemed like the right time. Besides, until Josie, I never met a woman I wanted to be with for more than a night—"

"Nunu!"

Ms. Baker laughs. "While I am truly amused at this situation, we need to get moving."

"Wait, what exactly is going on?"

"Pah," Nunu says, meaning, *"Oh sure, now you ask. It wasn't exactly a priority question when you learned I was gay, you little shit."*

"The basic rundown," Ms. Baker says, "is that your mission was hijacked, they threw you and the other settlers into cryo-sleep, and they tried to ransom you for more money that the Earth has to give."

"It was never about the money," Nunu spits.

"That's your theory, baby," Ms. Baker says.

"So, wait, how long have I been asleep?"

Nunu puts a hand on my shoulder and squeezes. "Four years."

"Four...FOUR YEARS?"

"Shhh," they both hiss.

"I've been asleep for four years?" I hiss back.

Nunu nods. "It took our crew a long time to catch up to you, even longer to figure out how to rescue you."

"Speaking of the crew," Ms. Baker says, "Thelma and Regina are both late for check in."

"Gertie?"

"She's fine. She found a bank of frozen children passengers and she's awaiting further instructions."

The door behind me *whooshes* open. Before I can even turn around, Nunu has drawn one of the knives from her belt and thrown it across the room. It hits the man who'd just entered square in his eye, digging in deep with a squishy sound, and he falls forward into the room.

I look from my Nunu to the man, and back again. "What the fuck have you been doing for four years?"

"Knitting, mostly," she says, stepping over the body to retrieve her knife. "The assassin bit just sort of came back once I started doing it again, like muscle memory."

"Came back," I repeat.

She presses her lips into an almost smile. "You knew I worked for the government."

"Yeah, but like, I just thought you pushed papers, did your time, and got out, like everybody else."

"Remember when Uncle Sal would come pick me up in the middle of the night for hunting trips?" I nod and she says, "He was my handler."

"Holy shit," I mutter.

"I realize you may be in the middle of an existential crisis," Ms. Baker says, "but we need to figure out our next move. Bodies are starting to pile up."

"And who are these other women with you?" I ask, rudely ignoring my grandmother's wife.

"My knitting circle," Nunu says.

Ms. Baker shakes her head and says, "Ex-operatives, like your grandmother. The government called in a lot of us old folks when your ship was stolen and their new agents had fuck all idea on what to do about it. Eloise picked out her own crew when she realized they weren't going to be able to save you, and you've had a bunch of grandma assassins chasing you through outer space."

Nunu shrugs. "If you think I'm going to let my precious girl go without a fight, you're out of your damn head."

I close the gap between us and crush her against me. Four years of her struggling and me sleeping are gone in an instant, and the unknown things between us become background, and it's just me hugging the woman who raised me, the woman who would chase me through space to make sure I'm safe.

When I step back from her, my head is clear and I'm all business. "Where are we now?"

"Between the Kuiper Belt and Jupiter."

"Fuel should've expired ages ago."

"They stole a refinery ship. There's enough fuel to keep them going indefinitely."

"Any other ships?"

"A warship. We're not sure who they stole it from, because no one will own up to creating a death machine when we're supposed to have a universal peace treaty," Ms. Baker says.

"Any other hostages, besides this ship?"

Nunu winces. "Not that we know of. There have been reports of smaller crafts going missing, but nothing concrete."

"And we have no idea what these people want?"

Nunu and Ms. Baker share a look that seems to convey an argument they've had at least a dozen times. Pretty sure Nunu's stare wins, because she says, "I don't think they're people."

I look between the two women before asking, "I'm sorry, what?"

"Not Earthlings, anyway. I think they're from Saturn, or maybe Titan itself, and they're trying to keep us from taking over their world."

"But the outer planets are uninhabitable without terraforming," I say. "There's no way they've lived there without our detection."

"Or that's what they want us to believe."

"If that's true—and that's a BIG if—couldn't we just talk to them? We can tell them we mean no harm, try to work things out. I mean, that would be a huge discovery for us and could propel us forward by hundreds of years," I say, getting excited.

"We've tried talking to them," Nunu says. "Whether they're Earthlings or something else, they're completely hostile."

"Not completely. They put us in cryo rather than killing us."

"That's what I *been* saying," Ms. Baker mutters.

The door *whooshes* again. Nunu's hand flies to her belt, but stills when a little old waif of a woman comes through. Her voice is shaky with both age and emotion as she says, "They got Thelma."

Ms. Baker releases a string of curse words in combinations I've never heard before. Then she asks, "Dead?"

The woman, who I assume is the missing Regina they'd discussed earlier, shakes her head and says, "She was alive, last I saw her. They were taking her to the bridge."

"Should I tell Henry?" Ms. Baker asks.

"No," Nunu says. "He'll come in hot, and we need him in our cruiser, ready to take off if things get too dicey. Better to keep him in the dark until we know what's what."

"How many of them are running the ship?" I ask.

"More than a dozen, less than twenty," Regina says.

I nod. "Okay then. If we're going to save Thelma and the other passengers, we need to take them out. We should stick together, remove them one by one."

Nunu says, "You need to find a quiet place and hole up.

Better yet, I'll get you to Henry and the getaway ship. We can handle this."

"I know this ship better than any of you. And I might not be a trained assassin, but I know enough to handle myself."

She draws in a sharp breath, gives a terse nod, and says, "Okay then, let's do this."

———

WE SNEAK THROUGH THE SHIP WITH A STEALTH I NEVER imagined a herd of grannies could have. One at a time, the soldiers go down. Whether they're human or alien, I don't stop to look. They've been holding my crew as prisoners for the last four years, robbing children of the chance to grow up, so whatever they are, they're the bad guys. With the help of my grandma's knitting group, they're the dead guys.

We scour the corridors until we're certain none are left, and find Gertie to fill her in on the plan. We've only killed nine in the halls, so there's a chance we're heading to the bridge outgunned two to one. None of these firecrackers seem to care one bit.

The doors part before us. Before the baddies can take in the fullness of the elderly onslaught, the women are on them. From the corner of my eye, I watch Ms. Baker do a flying kick into the face of one of the men. Tiny Regina kicks a knee so hard the crunch echoes around us. Gertie, the baby of the group at seventy-two, has shot two of them before any of theirs has even drawn a weapon.

Then there's Nunu, running around the place like a bat out of hell. Her blades slash before her like extensions of her hands. I've never seen her like this before. In all the years I've known her, maybe this is the first time I'm actually *seeing* her.

I fight my own baddies, but there's nothing exciting about it. There's the usual adrenaline surge, the rush of endorphins at victory, but I don't have a special move like these old ladies who might as well be videogame characters.

Still, it feels good when I look up and see they're all safe, all well, and all standing above a bad guy who won't hurt anyone again.

Ms. Baker steps to the controls at the front of the ship—the ship I should have led to a settlement on Saturn four years ago—and presses the call button. "Marta, Lolly: anyone read me?"

"Loud and clear, Jojo," someone answers. "The warship is ours."

"Refinery copies, safe and secure, one casualty," another voice answers.

Nunu laces her fingers through mine and we stand there in silence, listening to the radio chatter as the women report back their victories. There's a narrow window at the front of the ship and outside I can see a couple of the moons of Jupiter orbiting the gas giant.

"You know, this isn't what I expected when I busted you out of that nursing home. Space-faring grannies wielding knives, kicking ass, and taking no prisoners? Never in my wildest dreams."

"Really?" she asks. "Because it's exactly what I thought."

She squeezes my hand and we stare off together, watching the moons, imagining the next adventure to come.

LET THE SUN IN

CHAPTER 1
LET THE SUN IN

You are sad today. Most days it rests like an ache in your belly, mild and manageable; but today it arcs from you in a rainbow of smoky gray, ashen pewter, lead speckled with pearl. You're bursting with monochrome while the rest of the world passes by in colors you can't see.

Your pajamas feel itchy against dry skin. It has been several days since you showered—you aren't sure how many equals *several,* because you don't actually remember when it was. Days blur together, making such things insignificant. Showering and eating and basic human interaction feels pointless when one day and the next are the same.

It's past noon, you think, as you watch light trickle through a crack at the edge of your room-darkening curtains. Hooking a finger around the heavy fabric, you pull it aside to see a bright afternoon aglow in spring sunshine.

You hate it.

You want rain. Not just a little sprinkle; no, you want a downpour that pelts fat drops against anyone who dares go outside, biting into exposed skin, sending their teeth chattering and their spirits plummeting until they feel as cold and empty as you.

And you can have that, because you are a goddess of rain.

The clouds come first, fast and dark and glorious. You watch as the water lashes down against your window. A part of you, very small and very deep, feels a prickle of delight at the sight of people on the street below your window running for cover. The brief flicker of joy is not enough to brighten your spirit, and you sink back into your nest of comforters, burrowing in until the darkness pulls you back into unconsciousness.

At some point you wake and find yourself on the couch. You don't remember the exodus that brought you here, but that is not surprising. You often rouse and find yourself in unexpected places, like the sofa, and work, and leaning against Nani's gravestone.

You pick up your phone and speed-dial the only number saved. It rings once before a kind old voice asks, "The usual?"

"As fast as you can," you say before disconnecting the call and returning to your current priority—staring at the divot in the sage-green wall.

———

Zào Jūn lets himself into your apartment. You don't know how long it has been since you called, but the wall's dimple hasn't moved, and that's what matters.

He places the food on the table and sits by your feet, opening containers of shrimp lo mein, kung pao chicken, and egg foo young. You sit up and unwrap a plastic fork, stabbing an eggroll and biting off the end, not bothering with plates.

Zào Jūn kicks off his shoes as you click on the tv and ask, "*Bewitched* or *Murder She Wrote*?"

Zào Jūn mutters something that you don't understand, though you're half-sure it was a curse word. He says, "I should have known when the rain tasted like egg drop soup. I hate it when you're in a *Murder She Wrote* mood."

"Me too, Zào Jūn. Me too."

———

WHEN A SLIVER OF SUN CUTS ACROSS YOUR EYES ON ANOTHER morning—maybe the next morning, maybe days later— you're resolved to fix your curtains. You plan it in your head, sort through how and where to move the fabric, while remaining as still as possible in your blankets. The light moves away from your eyes and you decide you can worry about the curtains later, after a nap.

Hunger pangs in your gut and you crawl out of bed to speed-dial dinner again. A knock on the door disrupts your spot-staring. Zào Jūn never knocks. He has a key.

You look out the peephole at a small woman with a curtain of black hair shielding her face. You crack the door and accuse, "You're not Zào Jūn."

The woman looks up, a small smile on pale pink lips. She pushes past you, saying, "He sent me instead."

You inhale the sweet smell of jasmine, honeysuckle, and Korean barbecue. Your breath feels heavy in your lungs, your mouth stuffed with cotton balls. You barely manage, "Who are you?"

"Nahara."

She kicks off her shoes and plops onto the couch, picking up the tv remote. "There's a *Golden Girls* marathon tonight."

You almost smile. "I'll get us some plates."

———

NAHARA STAYS FOR FOUR DAYS THAT DON'T BLEED TOGETHER, and it doesn't rain once.

On the fifth day, she raises her head from the crook of your arm and throws the blankets off herself. "Okay, I'm leaving."

You don't say anything, as you've been waiting for this. You don't want her to go, but in the end, everyone does.

Nahara crawls toward you, brushes dark strands from your eyes, and presses her mouth against yours. It isn't a movie kiss—all lips and tongue and heavy breathing—but it is luxurious.

She climbs from your nest and pulls on her clothes and boots. You finally get the nerve to ask, "Will I see you again?"

Her smile dazzles, but she doesn't answer. With a shrug, Nahara leaves, taking all the colors in the room with her. When you hear the door bang shut, the rain begins.

———

ZÀO JŪN COMES TO VISIT AFTER DAYS OF NON-STOP RAIN. You don't even have to call him; he knows he is needed. He brings hot and sour soup with crispy wontons and dumplings, puts his arm around you while you binge *Perry Mason*.

He squeezes your shoulder when he catches you staring off again. "There is more to this room than the spot on the wall. You just need to look up."

"What's the point?"

You feel him shrug as he says, "A different view."

Taking a deep breath, you look up, because Zào Jūn wants you to. There's a bookcase and a lamp and a...a flower? Where did that come from? It is pale pink, the same shade as Nahara's lips.

"She left."

Zào Jūn squeezes your shoulder again. "She could come back, but she might not."

"When she looks at me, I feel sunlight on my face. I want her to fix me."

"It isn't about *fixing* you, dear one. You have to give yourself room to breathe, offer yourself a little kindness."

"I don't know how."

"Every day, little by little, you let the sun in."

———

IT HAS BEEN NEARLY TWO WEEKS SINCE YOU ATE DUMPLINGS WITH Zào Jūn. Sometimes the morning is fuzzy and you wait until it crystalizes into afternoon; some afternoons are made for napping, no matter how much you try to fight it. Still, you've made it to evening for thirteen days in a row. You know that, which is a victory in itself.

You have taken four showers in that time, worn clothes that aren't pajamas, and cooked three meals for yourself—two of them being grilled cheese, but they still count. You don't do this everyday, can't do this everyday, but it's a start. Sometimes you still want to stay in bed, and that's okay. You move your toes toward the curtain and let in the light. It may only be a sliver, but it is enough to remind you that the sun is still shining.

You've given yourself permission to make mistakes and find they're no longer debilitating. The feeling is not freeing, but it does loosen your chains a bit. Maybe someday those restraints will come off, but that is not something you think about now. Instead, you focus on each day, or each hour, or each minute, choosing to live for yourself.

Sometimes you still crave the rain, and that's okay. Without it, nothing grows.

———

YOU'RE READING A BOOK OF YOUR GRANDMOTHER'S FAVORITE poetry when there's a knock on the door. You look out at a curtain of dark hair, a shy smile, and with a smile of your own, you let the sun in.

TAP

CHAPTER 1

Jordan pulled his jacket around his face. The March air bit his skin, leaving his cheeks red and his brown eyes watering. He gazed up at the building, counting the windows to Gene's apartment. There was movement behind the floral curtain, and Jordan was sure Gene was lurking by the window, anxious for an explanation.

As he stepped off the sidewalk to cross the street, the sound of running footsteps caught Jordan's attention. He turned toward the sound. A dark-haired figure hurtled toward him, throwing their body over his and knocking him to the ground. Jordan struggled to sit up, but the figure grabbed him under his armpits and dragged him into an alleyway. A cat screeched and darted away as Jordan was shoved behind a row of trashcans. A calloused hand covered his mouth, and Jordan could taste salt and the tang of oranges.

Jordan caught the skin of the person's middle finger between his teeth and bit down as hard as he could.

"Fuck, that hurt."

Jordan spun toward the man. "Jesus Christ, Vic. You scared the hell outta me!"

Vic shushed him. "Keep your voice down."

"What's going on?"

"I don't know exactly," Vic whispered. "I was at the diner when I heard Gene's address go out over some cop's radio."

"Holy shit. He might be in trouble."

Vic nodded, his black hair falling into his eyes. "Us too."

Jordan turned back to the apartment building, his eyes wide. "You think this is about Reeva?"

"What else?" Vic asked with a shrug.

"We gotta help Gene."

Jordan pushed himself up from the sticky spot behind the trashcans, but Vic dragged him back down when they heard the sirens. Four police cars pulled up in front of Gene's building. The officers filed through the front door, guns drawn. Jordan and Vic stared up at Gene's apartment window in silence as the seconds ticked by.

Tic.

Tic.

Tic.

A shot rang out.

Blood spattered the curtain.

A stocky middle-aged man lifted the window and crawled onto the fire escape. Snippets of angry phrases followed him past the dirty glass, swirling to the ground like autumn leaves in a gale. Jordan barely registered the words. His eyes were locked on Gene.

"He's still wearing his work clothes," Jordan whispered.

Gene ignored the guns that had followed him through the window as he looked down at the street five stories below. He took a deep breath and raised his arms in front of his body.

Gene had always been a great swimmer. He'd won medals in high school that remained his pride and joy to this day. Now, as he threw himself from the fire escape, his arms outstretched in a swan dive, Gene's smile was unmistakable.

THE CRACK OF GENE'S HEAD WHEN IT HIT THE GROUND SOUNDED like the splitting of a rotten jack-o-lantern. It was immediately followed by a loud thud when the rest of his body caught up, and a sickening crunch when other bones broke upon impact. The perverse song of Gene's death played over and over in Jordan's head, an earworm he would never shake. He knew Vic was hearing it as well, because both of them stared in slack-jawed silence at the bloody carcass that was once their friend.

Vic came to his senses first. "We've gotta move."

"But Gene—"

"No," Vic said, cutting him off. "Gene's gone. Those cops ain't. They'll be swarming this place in no time."

Jordan ran his hand through his hair. "My place then."

"Are you out of your goddamned mind? We can't go to your place. Mine either. We can't go anywhere they might be expecting us."

"You're right," Jordan said, shaking his head. "I'm not thinking clearly."

"We'll figure it out as we go."

They stood to leave. Turning, they realized there was a red-haired man standing behind them. Thick arms were folded across his chest as he asked, "What are you doing to my trash cans?"

Jordan blinked twice, trying to work out the man's question through his heavy accent. He couldn't think of a plausible excuse, so he said, "Hiding." He hooked his thumb over his shoulder toward the police cars in the street behind them. He was almost certain he heard Vic's eyes roll, but the stranger just nodded.

"Alley becomes dead end. Come. Hide inside until they leave."

"We don't want to put you out," Jordan replied.

The man snorted. "Police are no friends to me."

Jordan followed the man to the backdoor of a small

restaurant's kitchen, but Vic grabbed his arm before he went in. In a quiet, rushed tone, he asked, "What are you doing? You don't know this guy. He could turn us in as soon as we go inside."

"I don't think he will," Jordan said.

"Your thinking hasn't done much for us lately," Vic grumbled.

Jordan tensed. "I know. This is my fault. You'd both be fine if I hadn't told you about the water."

"You didn't know. You couldn't have," Vic said.

A woman's voice came from inside, sharp and authoritative. "Don't just stand there letting the cold in."

Jordan ducked his head in apology as she came into view. She was a slip of a woman, with limp brown hair graying at her temples. Jordan stepped inside, Vic close behind. Vic pushed out a long breath through his teeth before muttering, "Fuck it."

"We don't talk like that in this place, mister," the woman said.

She moved past them and pulled the door shut, glaring at the big man as she did.

"Sorry, Zoya," he said.

She sighed. "No, Fedya, you're not. You love taking in strays."

Jordan watched Fedya squirm under Zoya's gaze, his cheeks going red. "Strays keep the mice away."

"Or they call down the catcher's net."

"They were in trouble."

"And we will be in trouble if they're found," she replied.

"We don't want to be a problem for you," Jordan said.

Zoya waved his words away as a cough racked her body. "Everything is a problem these days."

Fedya handed her a glass of water and she tipped it back greedily. Jordan's thoughts turned to Reeva as another fit of coughing overtook Zoya. Reeva's illness started as a cough.

"We should phone a doctor," Fedya whispered. "Three weeks you've had this cough."

"The doctors won't come without the rash. The virus is their only concern, not the cough of some old woman."

"You're forty-three, Zoya. You shouldn't feel like an old woman."

"Forty-three," she said, shaking her head in disbelief. She leaned over the stainless steel counter and grumbled, "The years have felt much longer."

All four heads jerked up as the door jingled open at the front of the restaurant.

Fedya tensed. "I'll go. Hide them."

Zoya stood immobile as Fedya pushed through to the front room. As soon as he was gone, she burst into motion. She grabbed Jordan and Vic by the sleeves, directing them up the narrow stairs along the back wall. They stumbled into a dim room partitioned by yellowed bed sheets.

Zoya ushered them to the back corner where the walls met. She slipped her fingers into a thin crack and pulled back a panel of the wall.

"Inside," she hissed.

Vic pushed himself behind the wall, Jordan following behind. Just as Jordan slipped inside, a soft voice from behind one of the sheets asked, "Mama?"

Zoya released the panel of the wall, leaving Jordan and Vic in darkness. Jordan felt Vic shuddering beside him as he plucked at strands of spider webs tickling his face. Jordan slipped past Vic toward a narrow break in the wood that let him see a sliver of the room. He watched Zoya's shadow dance across the sheet as she sat on a bed beside a frail body.

"I'm here, Dimitri."

Her ferocity was gone the moment she said his name. Jordan blinked back the tears at the sudden recognition of what was happening. A knot formed in his throat as he whispered, "It's the water."

"You don't know that," Vic whispered back, but Jordan could hear the hesitation in his voice.

"It's killing them. How many families are suffering because of it?"

They watched in silence as Zoya's shadow stroked her son's hair. When she lifted her head and looked toward the stairs, Jordan's eyes followed her gaze. Fedya's head bobbed into view, his face as red as his hair. As he emerged into the room, Jordan saw the reason for his alarm: two officers trailed behind him, guns drawn.

Zoya was on her feet in an instant, moving outside the makeshift room and closing the sheets to shield Dimitri. "Why do you think you can bring your guns into my home?" she asked.

"Zoya—" Fedya trailed off, but his eyes were pleading for silence.

The officers left Fedya standing by the stairs as they searched behind each curtain. When they reached the room where Dimitri slept, Zoya stepped in front of them and said, "You will put your guns away before you go near my son."

"Hold her," one said as he moved toward Dimitri's room.

His partner grabbed Zoya's arms and held her back, but his expression was full of apology. The lead officer tore down the sheets, then moved to stand over Dimitri. In one swift move, he ripped the blankets off the boy. Dimitri whimpered and tucked his body into a ball as if to hide from the stranger standing over him.

"Stop this," Zoya yelled. "We obey the laws. We pay our taxes. We stay within the zones. You have no right."

"My *pchelka*, please. Let them do what they must," Fedya said.

The officer holding Zoya looked at her sheepishly. "I'm sorry, ma'am. We're just following orders."

"Orders," she repeated. Zoya turned her head and spat on the ground.

"Shut her up, McCoy, or I'll do it for you."

McCoy said, "There's nothing here, Deke. Let's get moving."

Deke moved through the room with unearned confidence. "They're hiding something."

"She's got a sick kid. She's worried. That's it," McCoy replied.

Deke sneered as he stepped toward Zoya. He lifted his gun toward her head and said, "Don't force my hand, woman. What are you hiding?"

"Man, come on. Let's check next door."

Zoya stared at the barrel of the gun. Leaning forward so her forehead touched the metal, she said, "Do it."

Deke shifted the gun toward Dimitri.

"No," she stammered, all bravado lost.

The safety clicked off.

Fedya dived toward the cop. Deke swung his gun toward Fedya, but the big man knocked it away with little effort. As Fedya swung his fist toward the officer, a blast echoed off the low ceiling.

Jordan watched the whole thing as if in slow motion. His ears were filled with ringing, his body pulsating with the intensity of the shot as it vibrated through the room. He saw blood blossoming on Fedya's shirt. Jordan's gaze flicked to McCoy, hands shaking as he stared at the gun in his shaking hand.

Fedya slipped to his knees as Zoya ran to him. She turned to the officer, her eyes wide in horror.

"I didn't mean to," McCoy stuttered.

Fedya looked to Zoya and said, "Don't be angry with them."

Jordan saw Fedya's eyes shift toward the wall where they hid and knew he wasn't talking about the police.

"Call it in," Deke said as he handcuffed Zoya. "We'll process this one for obstruction."

McCoy walked back toward the stairs, his voice muffled as he talked into his radio. Deke whispered to Zoya, "*You* did this, you obstinate bitch."

Jordan saw all the fight go out of Zoya and she slumped to the floor in another coughing fit. Deke chuckled as he walked to the stairs where McCoy had gone to call for backup. His head disappeared below as the shrill cry of sirens blared in the distance.

Zoya looked toward the wall. The sadness was so heavy on her face it was tangible. "Why are they searching for you?"

Jordan pressed his face against the wood and whispered, "Don't drink the water. You and your son will get better as soon as you stop drinking it."

"Why?" she asked.

"Please," Jordan said. "Just trust me."

"Trust you," she scoffed. But a second later she nodded and said, "Don't come out until dark. Give Dimitri the milk from downstairs before you leave. I'll send someone for him as soon as I can."

"What will happen to you?" Jordan asked.

She shrugged. "It doesn't matter anymore."

"This is my fault."

He looked to Zoya for forgiveness, but none was there. When he heard footsteps on the stairs, silence fell between them and he knew his penance would never be enough.

CHAPTER 2

E very footfall on the pavement sounded like Gene's body hitting the ground.

Jordan heard it echoing through the alleys as they ran, seeking sanctuary in the shadows. He heard it in the silence as they stilled for a cruiser to pass. He heard it with each breath he took, each breath Gene didn't take.

"Stop," Vic whispered. He threw his hand out in front of Jordan, grabbing his shirt and pulling him to a stop.

Jordan looked up. Through tear-filled eyes he saw a bleary light flashing in the street in front of him. He wiped at his eyes and looked down at his hand in confusion when he saw the wet streak across his knuckle. How long had he been crying?

"No sirens," Vic said. "It's a plague truck."

They huddled in the alley out of sight, waiting for the truck to leave. After several minutes, four figures in chem-suits trudged through the street, each wheeling a body toward the truck. The bodies were still, not dead, but silent as the grave. The coughing fits and fever that marked the first symptoms had passed and these bodies were now in the waking coma that brought the death collectors to their doors.

Vic was tugging on Jordan's jacket, backing away for fear

they would catch the plague. Jordan stared on, watching them load the bodies onto the truck before they climbed inside to leave.

The speculation that the plague was airborne had been worrisome at first; in fact, Jordan himself had worn a face-mask the first few weeks the rumors had swirled, hoping to be protected while he walked to the factory.

Now he knew better. It wasn't in the air; it was in the water.

"They're gone," he said.

"We should be, too," Vic muttered. "You don't want to risk—"

"Exposure?" Jordan interrupted. He laughed, a short, clipped sound.

Vic nodded tersely. "Just in case."

Jordan leaned his forehead against the old brownstone's alley wall and clasped his hands behind his head, using his elbows to block out the world. He sat there for a long moment before Vic cleared his throat and said, "Hey man, we gotta go."

"Yeah," Jordan said, turning around. He walked toward the street where the plague truck had been, though Vic was slow to follow. "You know it's clear, Vic. No one who saw the lights will walk this street until morning."

"Maybe we shouldn't either."

Jordan stepped into the street. He turned to face Vic, still standing at the edge of the buildings. "Come on. Reeva's journal told us how they're getting sick, and it's not exposure."

"What if she was wrong? What if it was just the ravings of..." he trailed off.

Jordan was in Vic's face in an instant, jabbing his index finger against Vic's chest. "She was sick, not crazy. They're not the same thing."

"We don't know what the sickness does, J. Maybe the sickness made her hallucinate and write those things about the water."

"Explain away her writings all you want, blame the sickness, say she was delusional," Jordan said. "But you can't explain how she got better when she stopped drinking it."

Vic took a deep breath, weighing his words before he spoke. His voice was soft when he said, "Could be the last stage. The collectors come before it gets to that point. Maybe they do it to prevent loved ones from hoping their people are getting better before they, you know."

"Die."

It wasn't just a word, it was a pronouncement. A verdict. A possibility Jordan wasn't ready to consider yet. Reeva wasn't dead, she was just…gone.

She had disappeared and he needed to know why.

Jordan's thoughts turned to the first time he saw her. He was walking down the hall to his apartment when he heard the most terrible, blood-curdling screeches. He ran to her open door, prepared to fight whatever was attacking her. But it was just a girl, a beautiful girl, standing on a ladder, more paint on her than on the brush in her hand, and she was singing along to whatever song blared through her headphones. He'd laughed until his face hurt, then helped her paint her new apartment.

He'd give anything to hear her awful singing now.

Jordan turned away from Vic and started across the street. He knew Vic didn't want Reeva to be dead. No one did. She was a bright light in a dark world.

"I'm sorry," Jordan said.

"Nah man, I'm the one who should be sorry." Vic paused, looked away. He raked his tongue across his teeth, then looked at his shoes. He whispered, "You know I loved her, too, right?"

Jordan ground his teeth together before forcing out, "I know."

Thunder rumbled in the distance. A cascade of lightning awakened along the horizon. It flashed over the white tents outside the fence, outside the safety zones, where death lived.

"We need to find shelter before the rain comes," Vic said.

He was right, of course. Everyone knew the rain was dangerous, corrosive against flesh. But Jordan didn't know where to go. He said, "We have some money saved, not much, but we could rent a room."

"We can't let a merchant scan your chip or the cops will know where we are. We'll need to get all your cash at once and in a hurry."

"Cash is suspicious," Jordan said.

"Not if we go to the Crumbs. Less cops patrolling there, too."

"Because they've given up on the place," Jordan said. He pressed his lips into a tight line as he considered it, then nodded his consent. "Is there a cash tank nearby?"

Vic's blue eyes were lit by another flash of lightning, closer. He looked at their surroundings, taking stock. "Corner of Fifth and Fourteenth, beside the police station."

Jordan scoffed. "We can't go there."

"It's the closest. And it's on the way to the Crumbs."

A sudden clap of thunder made Jordan jump. He looked out over the plague tents and said, "I guess we don't have a choice. Lead the way."

———

THEY STOOD ACROSS THE STREET FROM THE CASH TANK, WATCHING the police officers moving in and out of the station. There seemed to be an abundance of them entering in their basic uniforms, while those who trickled out were covered in heavy protective gear, without the tiniest scrap of skin showing.

"They're getting ready for the rain," Vic said. "The patrols will die down until it's over and the street washers can clear it away."

Jordan put his hands on his hips. With a sigh he said, "Too bad we can't use that time."

Vic nodded, but his eyes never left the police station. "They're leaving about every four minutes. I can track that pretty well. But I can't account for the ones going in."

"They're more worried about getting in before the rain hits," Jordan said. "Let's go when the next one leaves."

They watched, Vic counting the seconds as they waited. Three minutes and fifty-six seconds. They stepped out of the alley and crossed the street. Jordan's gait was quick, but Vic grabbed his shoulder and slowed him down.

"Keep it casual, J."

Jordan nodded. He stepped to the cash tank while Vic rounded the corner and leaned against the wall, a mere five feet from the station's entrance.

Jordan swiped his hand under the chip reader. The machine beeped twice, an error filling the screen with blocky red letters.

INSUFFICIENT FUNDS.

No, Jordan thought, *that's not right.*

He swiped his hand again. Error. He pounded his fist against the tank, accompanied by a string of expletives. Jordan stepped back from the machine and rounded the corner where Vic waited, having a smoke.

Through gritted teeth, Jordan said, "It's not working."

"Damnit," Vic said. "Lemme try."

They stood by the tank, watching the error flash as Vic ran his hand under the reader. Jordan said, "Maybe the machine's out."

"They flagged us, dipshit," Vic said. "We gotta get outta here."

They stepped across the street in the direction of the

Crumbs. They'd only gone a block when a cop in his basics turned the corner in front of them.

"Keep walking," Vic whispered. "He's in a hurry to get to the station before the rain."

As the officer approached, they each nodded a greeting. The cop's brow furrowed and he said, "You'd better get inside. The rain's coming."

Jordan felt his heart stop at the sound of the man's voice. *Shit shit shit shit.*

"Yessir," Vic said. "That's where we're headed."

Vic elbowed Jordan. "Right," Jordan said. "You be safe out there."

They kept walking. A block away, Vic asked, "Be safe out there?"

Jordan winced in apology. "It's all I could think of."

"You know who that was," Vic said.

Jordan nodded. "He killed Fedya."

They walked in silence until they reached the Crumbs. Though the buildings had grown increasingly worse as they'd walked toward the city's outskirts, the dilapidated structures of the Crumbs could hardly be classified as buildings. Busted windows, doors falling from hinges, walls full of holes—and eyes staring out of each. The people living in the Crumbs watched every step Jordan and Vic took, not hostilely, at least not openly, but with caution and a readiness to protect what little they had.

Vic pointed out a small structure, barely standing, that looked empty. They crossed the street toward it as the sound of rain on the street filled their ears.

"Run!" Jordan yelled.

Vic threw himself against the door, forcing it open. Jordan tumbled in behind him and slammed the splintered wood closed. There was a hole in the ceiling in the middle of the room and water fell on the dusty floor in fat drops.

They moved to the corner of the room that seemed to be

the furthest from the hole in the ceiling. Vic picked up a pile of dirty rags and tossed them in the corner to sit on. Jordan slid down the wall and pulled his knees to his chin. They listened to the rain for a few minutes before Jordan asked, "What now?"

"If we're lucky, we wait here until the cleanup crews clear the rain." He leaned his head back and closed his eyes. It wasn't long before his breathing became a low rumble of snores next to Jordan's ear.

Jordan stared up at the hole in the ceiling, watching the rain pour upon the earth. With a sigh he said, "We're not lucky."

CHAPTER 3

The rain lasted most of the night and into early morning. Jordan kept watch until sheer exhaustion and the syncopated drip of water lulled his eyes closed. He woke just before dawn, when the pale morning light was beginning to sift through the darkness. But it wasn't the light that woke him; it was the overpowering silence. The absence of sound was a noise itself.

He glanced to his right. Vic was still asleep beside him, his black hair loose and falling over his face. Jordan wasn't sure how his friend could sleep so easily after everything that had happened, but he dare not wake him from his reprieve. If he could escape this nightmare through sleep, so be it.

Jordan stood and skirted the room until he reached the broken door. He peaked through one of the many cracks, his eyes searching the street outside.

"Cleanup crews won't come through for another fifteen minutes."

Jordan spun toward the voice. Gravelly. Feminine. A voice full of fire.

His eyes searched the shadows in the corners of the room until he found her. Against the far wall, a pile of dirty blankets with a head full of wild ruby curls was staring at him.

"We didn't know anyone was here," Jordan said.

"Better for both of us that way," she said. "If you'd found me, I would have cast you into the rain."

"Why tell me now? Why not just wait for us to leave?"

"I want to make sure that's what you plan to do. You can't be here once the streets are clear."

"Why?"

She unwrapped herself from her blankets and moved closer to the hole in the ceiling, closer to the light.

"Because I don't want to kill you today."

Jordan could see her clearly now; she was covered in grime and grit, tattered from head to toe, but it didn't diminish her ferocity. If anything, it strengthened it. Her voice was emotionless, her words simple. She spoke without bravado or threat, but with honesty. She was willing to kill him if she needed to, though Jordan had no idea why she thought she might.

"I don't know who you think we are—"

"Spare me," she said, rolling her eyes. "I heard the rovers out all night running through the Crumbs. They don't come here unless they're lookin' for someone. Especially when it's raining. So whatever you did must've been pretty bad."

Jordan shook his head. "We didn't do anything."

She laughed, but there was no joy in it. "None of us did. We just like the aesthetic of this shithole. That's why we hide in rubble and trade in favors."

"I know how it looks," he said.

"Guilty," she said. "But I'm not here to judge you. I'm here to survive. And I can't do that if you bring the cops with you."

Jordan sighed. Guilt or innocence didn't matter in a place like this. All that mattered was whether or not there would be a tomorrow. That's why they called it the Crumbs. The people had learned to live on little more.

"We'll leave as soon as they scrub the streets."

She nodded. "Wake your friend. I want you out as soon as they leave. And tell that bastard to give my blankets back."

————

THE MORNING WAS COOL, UNCOMFORTABLY SO. REEVA WOULD'VE loved it. She always said the cold gave her an excuse to get into the coffee rations without feeling bad. Jordan never understood that. He didn't like coffee. Now he craved it.

"We need food," Vic said, drawing him back to the moment. "And wat—" he started, but caught himself and threw his hands up to ward off a lecture. "I know. We can't drink the water. Something else to drink, then."

Jordan's sharp brown eyes met his. "But you're right, we need to eat. I'm just not sure where to go."

Vic ducked out from under the overhang where they were hiding and motioned Jordan to follow. As they crossed the street, he said, "I've been thinking about that. We know they're watching your place, and probably mine, but it might be safe to go to Mom's."

"No way. They'd expect us to go there."

Vic moved to stand inside a shoddy doorway, hidden in shadows. "Not if they've done their research. Mom and I haven't been on good terms for a long time."

"I know," Jordan said, running his hand over his too-long hair. "That's another reason we can't go to Gloria's. Not after the way she treated you. It's not right."

"She's an old woman, J. She doesn't get it. And I've learned to accept that about her, even if she hasn't learned to accept me."

"You can't really want to drag her into this."

Vic shrugged. "I mean, right now we're only wanted for questioning. Maybe they're waiting for us to turn ourselves in. Maybe we *should* turn ourselves in"

Jordan stared at Vic, his lips moving though no words

came out. When his voice finally found itself, he asked, "Did you forget what happened yesterday? What they did to Gene?"

"We don't know what happened in that apartment," Vic said. "And you saw Gene. He wasn't forced over. He jumped."

Jordan yelled, "There had to be a reason for that!"

As soon as the words left his mouth, he knew he'd made a mistake. Skulking through alleys only works if you're quiet.

"Let's go," Vic said. He walked deeper into the shadows, glancing over his shoulder every few steps.

"You there. Stop!"

They both turned toward the voice. A cop was standing at the alley entrance; his hand rested on the gun at his right hip while he radioed with his left. His eyes never left them.

"We gotta keep going, Vic."

"He'll shoot us if we move," Vic said.

"He'll shoot us if we don't."

Jordan took a small step back. The cop's voice dropped to a growl. "Don't. Move."

"I'm sorry," Jordan said.

He bolted.

Vic cursed, then shot off after him. The cop was on their heels, puffing into his radio as they ran. There would be more, soon.

Jordan zigzagged through two more alleys before he heard the sirens. He turned and dashed into a third alley. There was a fence at the end. If he tried to climb, they'd shoot him. It wasn't a guess; he knew it, could feel it in his bones.

"Time to stop," Vic panted.

"Your friend is right," the cop said. "It's over. Come with me peacefully before this gets out of hand."

"It already has."

He recognized the gravel in her voice the moment before he saw her hand slice the throat of the cop, before the officer fell to the ground, revealing her standing there with eyes like embers.

The tattered blankets were gone, replaced with a fitted black top and jeans. Her grimy face was wiped clean and covered in freckles. Her hair though, wild ruby curls spiraling out from her face, that hadn't changed.

"You," Jordan whispered.

"Enough of the pleasantries," she said, moving past him. "Let's move."

"Whoa, wait a sec. Who the fuck are you?" Vic asked.

Jordan elbowed him. "It's the girl I told you about, from this morning."

"Yeah?" Vic asked. Turning to the girl he said, "That still doesn't answer my question."

She put her hands on her hips and said, "We don't have time for this."

"Make time," Vic said.

"My name is Keelan. I'm trying to save your worthless asses."

Jordan asked, "Why?"

"That's what I want to know," Vic said, crossing his arms.

Keelan raked her tongue over her teeth. She and Vic stared hard at one another, a battle raging in their gazes. Vic must have won, because Keelan sighed and turned to Jordan, saying, "Because it's what she would want me to do."

Jordan felt his heart miss a beat. His voice was little more than a whisper when he asked, "Who?"

"Reeva. She's alive."

CHAPTER 4

live.

The word wasn't big enough. It didn't explain the way her left eye squinted when she smiled. It couldn't describe the smell of soap on her skin, somehow sweeter than anything else he'd ever smelled. The little word meant that she was breathing, being, but it didn't tell of the way she held her breath when she was lying, only to let it out in one big rush when she inevitably told the truth.

Though it wasn't big enough to say any of these things, it was enough to fill Jordan with hope.

He jogged to catch up with Keelan. She'd been leading them through abandoned buildings, burned homes, and back alleys for a quarter of an hour. Jordan knew he and Vic couldn't have navigated the Crumbs without her. Moving alley to alley was easy enough, but she led them through a maze that made no sense to an outsider.

She stopped. Jordan skidded to a halt beside her. His mind was buzzing with questions about Reeva and her disappearance, but he knew he needed to be careful what he asked in case someone was listening. As Keelan peered around the corner to check the next corridor, Jordan asked, "So Reeva sent you to help us?"

Keelan glanced at him from the side of her eye. "Not exactly."

She took a step, but Jordan grabbed her sleeve and pulled her back. "What do you mean 'not exactly?'"

Keelan pressed her lips into a thin line. She turned to face him, her green eyes meeting his. "She sent me for the journal."

"Then why did you help us?" Vic asked, suspicion clear in his tone.

"Accident," Keelan said with a shrug. "I realized who you were when I heard you talking before you left the shack. I followed you, just in case. Even though I wasn't sent to get you, doesn't mean Reeva would want you arrested."

Jordan felt as if she'd punched him in the gut. He forced the words out, needing to hear them aloud: "She left the journal for me, so I could figure this out. So I could help her."

"No," she said, shaking her head. "She forgot it when she fled."

He bit his lip until he tasted metal. "She didn't want me to find her."

Keelan put her hand on his arm. "Don't let this get into your head. It isn't that she doesn't care about you, she didn't want you entangled in this mess."

"So, what, better I wonder if she's dead?" he asked, his voice trailing away in a manic laugh.

Vic put his arm around Jordan's shoulders. "She was trying to protect you."

Jordan shook his arm off. "She did a shitty job."

Keelan eyed him a moment longer before turning back to the path. She led them the rest of the way in silence. When they emerged out of the twisting passages and onto the edge of a main street, they were only half a block from Jordan's apartment.

Keelan said. "I count four cops. There may be more inside. Depends on how bad they want you."

"Four?" Vic asked.

Jordan scanned the street. "I don't see any."

She smirked and rolled her eyes. "Newspaper stand, tan suit. Stoop, red cap. Parked car on the right. Lady on the bench."

"No way. You're just picking out random people," Jordan said.

"You can chance it if you don't believe me," she said, "or I'll go get the journal myself. Reeva gave me her keys. I'll be in and out."

Jordan rubbed his hands over his face. "Keys won't work. I had a chip lock installed after she disappeared."

"You're shitting me," she said, putting her fingers over the bridge of her nose.

He winced. "I guess I'm going with you."

She huffed. "Fine, but not like that." She pointed her finger at his clothes and said, "We'll need to do something about all this. Follow me."

She turned back down the alley, leading them back into the labyrinth.

———

THE MARKET WAS A HODGEPODGE OF HALF-BUILDINGS AND TENTS cobbled together to create a home for the tinkerers, conmen, and thieves that sold and traded to the denizens of the Crumbs.

Keelan led them toward a shop with a stocky woman leaning on an oak walking stick. Before they'd reached her, the woman's green eyes were already watching—no, more than that—judging the stuff they were made of.

She puckered her lips in contempt and said, "What do you want, red?"

"Nice to see you too, Aysie."

Aysie shook her head, faint light catching the little silver buzzed hairs. "That's not what I fuckin' said."

Jordan tilted his head toward Keelan and whispered, "Maybe we should go."

"Maybe you should," Aysie said, her eyes fixing on him.

"Nah, she's gonna help us," Keelan said. "She always regales me with her charm when I first arrive. But she warms up once I show her what I've brought. Don't you, Aysie?"

Aysie snorted, but she didn't refute it. Instead she waved them through a frayed mustard-colored curtain into a small room full of an assortment of items. As Jordan stared at the objects before him, he noticed a few so strange he couldn't identify them.

"Put your eyes back in your head, boy," Aysie said. "My shit is for sale, not for gawking at."

"Don't mind him, he's new here," Keelan said.

Aysie laughed. It was a strange, sweet sound at odds with the rest of her. She said, "Anyone who looks at him can tell that. Both of them." Pointing at Vic she added, "At least that one has some darkness about him. I'd bet he's been in a pickle or two."

Vic's lip curled at one corner and he said, "A couple, yeah."

Aysie nodded at him appraisingly. Turning back to Keelan she said, "Show me what you brought."

Keelan rolled up her pant leg and unzipped her boot. She pulled out a silver dagger and handed it to Aysie. Switching legs, she produced three nutrition bars. She emptied her pockets, giving Aysie a couple of old coins, a box of matches, a pocket watch with a shattered face, and four rings with most of the stones intact.

The old lady eyed the items, doing figures in her head. "Not as much as last time."

"But more than enough for what I need."

"And what's that?"

Keelan swung her thumb over her shoulder and wiggled it between Jordan and Vic. "I need to hide these guys. And not just in the Crumbs. Plainclothes are watching the building we're casing."

Aysie's eyebrows quirked up. "Big job?"

"Could be," Keelan said with a shrug. "Take care of them and I'll keep my eyes out for you."

"Done," Aysie said. She spit in her hand and reached for Keelan. The girl returned the gesture, shaking Aysie's hand. Turning to the men, Aysie said, "Buckle up, boys. You're in for a ride. When I'm done, you won't even know yourselves."

———

JORDAN, VIC, AND KEELAN CROSSED THE STREET AND WALKED toward the apartment building. Though Keelan had cautioned him to keep his eyes on the building and ignore the cops who were watching, Jordan felt himself looking for the plainclothes from the corner of his eye.

They stepped into the foyer of the apartment without incident. Jordan smiled broadly and said, "We made it."

"Don't get too cocky," Keelan said. "We still have to get into your apartment, find what we need, and get out without attracting suspicion."

Jordan looked down at the pale blue dress he wore. "I really don't think anyone will recognize me."

"Are you kidding? You clopped across the street so awkwardly I was shocked no one stopped you," Vic said.

Jordan's cheeks went red. "I'm not used to these shoes."

"Vic did fine," Keelan said, smirking.

"Not my first time in heels, babe."

They took the elevator to the fifth floor. Keelan checked the hallway, but no one was there. They dashed to the door, Jordan sliding his wrist against the chip-reading panel. Slipping inside, they saw the apartment in shambles. Couch cushions were in the floor, clothes were strewn about, and books were piled haphazardly in front of the bookcase.

Keelan cursed. "They've ransacked the place."

They stood there a moment, staring at the mess, before Jordan sprang to action. He whipped off the wig and dress Aysie had put him in and rolled down the jeans he'd been wearing underneath. He slipped on nearby sneakers and said, "Vic, grab us some warm clothes and fill my backpack. It should be—"

"—in the closet," Vic finished, waving a dismissive hand. He headed for the bedroom, undressing as he went.

Jordan said, "Keelan, gather as much food as you think we can carry. We don't have long."

"It doesn't matter now," Keelan said. "If they got Reeva's journal, they know everything. We need to warn the others."

"They don't have her journal."

He walked to the doorframe between the front hall and the living room. Kneeling down, he pressed his thumbs against the wood frame and turned them left. The wood slid out of place, revealing a small compartment. Jordan reached inside and pulled out a thin leather book. He turned to Keelan and smiled, waving it at her.

She snickered. "You sonuvabitch. That's damn clever."

Jordan shrugged, tucking it into the back of his pants. "Maybe we're luckier than I thought."

"I wouldn't go that far."

Jordan and Keelan turned toward the voice. An officer was standing at the front door, his gun pointed at Jordan's head. Jordan knew the guy, recognized the awful sneer on his face.

Deke.

This was the asshole that pointed his gun at a sick child to try to get a mother to talk. He didn't pull the trigger when Fedya was shot, but it was his fault.

"Don't try to be a hero," Deke said. "We've got all the exits covered. They wanted to catch you when you left, but I wanted to be here and see the look on your face when you realized it was over."

"Look," Jordan said, "I don't know who you think we are—"

"Cut the shit, Adler. I know all about you and your lady friend. Where is she, anyway?"

"Reeva's gone. I filed a report at the station."

"Not her, dumbass. Where's Victoria Spencer?"

Vic slowly stepped out of the bedroom, a backpack slung over his shoulder, his hands in the air. "I'm here."

The cop sneered. "You don't look like the pretty girl in your mom's pictures."

Vic ground his teeth together and Jordan could see his restraint manifested in the tightness of his jaw and the clenching of his fists. In a tone strangled with anger, Vic replied, "My mother had a son. She just didn't know it."

"Whatever you say, sweetheart," Deke replied, rolling his eyes. He motioned with his gun and said, "All of you, start walking."

Vic, Jordan, and Keelan stepped into the hallway. Deke's partner, McCoy, was standing against the wall with his gun pointed at them.

"Told you it was them," Deke said as they entered the elevator.

"Sorry, man. I just couldn't—"

"You need to get your shit together," Deke said as he slid past them, putting himself against the back wall. "If you can't handle it anymore, you need to desk yourself."

"What's wrong?" Jordan asked. "Feeling bad for shooting an innocent man."

"Fuck off, Adler," Deke said. He motioned McCoy to stand beside him. Both officers held their guns in front of them as Deke said, "Face the door and put your hands above your heads." Deke pulled Reeva's journal from Jordan's waistband. "There'll be a fuck-ton of guns on you as soon as those doors open. I wouldn't move if I were you."

When the elevator stopped, they filed out into the foyer. Vic asked, "Where's that fuck-ton? Looks like you're on your own, lil fella."

Deke cursed, radioed in his successful capture, and asked where his backup was. When the muffled reply came, he said, "Shit. When did that start?"

Another staticky response. "Yeah, we're good til it stops. Over and out."

Jordan felt a grin break out across his face. He saw the rain beading on the cloudy glass of the apartment lobby. "What's wrong? Afraid of a little rain?"

"Funny. I guess you're gonna walk right out into it?"

Jordan chuckled and said, "Yeah, actually, I am."

"The hell you are," Vic said.

Jordan slowly turned so he was facing his friends and the cops. "Don't you see, Vic? Everything is a lie. They've been using the water to keep us under their thumbs. Give the masses poison to control them. The tap and the bottled waters are full of whatever they've been using. Take away the chance to get good water by convincing them the rain is dangerous. Hell, I stopped drinking the government rations two days ago, and already I can think more clearly."

He took a step backwards toward the door. Deke said, "Not another move, jackass."

"Or what?" Jordan asked. "You'll shoot me?"

"Or I really will let you go out there and burn your skin off. You fucking conspiracy psychos really piss me off."

Jordan backed closer to the door. "Here's the thing: if you take me to jail, I'm going to die. I don't know how you'll do it, but I know I won't come back out."

"You'll get out if you're innocent," McCoy said. "Just answer the questions, tell the truth, and you'll be fine."

Keelan sneered. "You can't really believe that."

"I do," McCoy said, glancing at Deke as if he needed confirmation.

"I don't," Jordan said.

He jumped for the front door, throwing it open and hurling himself into the rain. It fell against his bare chest in great freezing drops. Jordan held his arms out, looking at his soaked skin. Unhurt. Cold and pale as the water saturated every part of him, but he remained undamaged.

A grin spread across his face as Keelan and Vic ran out after him. Deke and McCoy followed outside, pausing under the great green awning on the front of the building. They shouted at them, brandishing their guns, but the trio kept running until the officers behind them were only a memory.

CHAPTER 5

"You sure about this?" Jordan asked.

Vic nodded. "I only need a minute."

"You don't need to prove your worth to Gloria," Jordan said. "And you don't owe her anything."

Vic sighed. "This may be the last time I ever see my mother. After the storm passes, the cops will regroup and probably have this place on lockdown. I just...I need to say goodbye. Not for her. For me."

"Whatever you're doing, do it fast," Keelan said as she glanced about. "We don't have time for this."

Jordan ignored her, putting his hand on Vic's shoulder. "Whatever you need, man. I'm here for you."

The three walked into the building, ignored reception, and marched down the hall to his mother's room. Vic held his knuckles to the door and paused. He took a deep breath and released it, then thumped on the door.

They heard noise inside, then grumbling from behind the door. A tall woman with slumped shoulders cracked open the door. She peered outside through wire-rimmed spectacles, her pale green eyes dull behind them. The hallway's fluorescent lights filtered over her silver hair, causing it to glow like a halo around her wrinkled face.

"Whatever you're selling, I don't want," she said. She moved her hand to close the door, but Vic stuck his foot in the crack to hold it open.

"We're not selling anything."

Her eyes searched his face for someone she recognized. After a moment she whispered, "Vicky?"

"Just Vic, mom."

"Why are you wet?"

Vic shrugged. "We got stuck in the rain."

She inhaled sharply, looking him up and down for signs of damage. After a moment, she opened the door and turned her head side to side, checking the empty hallway. Turning back to them she said, "You'd better come inside."

The inside of Gloria Spencer's apartment looked like a garden exploded. Potted plants, trees, and a wide array of blossoms, both real and fake, surrounded flower-printed furniture draped in floral blankets and quilts. Gloria sat in a creaky white rocking chair and motioned for the others to sit across from her on the antique sofa.

"I wondered if you'd come," she said. Her eyes bore into Vic, searching him for whatever she was looking for. "I told the police you didn't visit your poor mother anymore."

Vic pressed his lips together for a moment before saying, "That's as much your decision as it is mine."

Gloria waved her hand dismissively. "What do you want from me? You're a stranger now."

"I'm the same. Why can't you see that?"

"I had a daughter!" Gloria said. "She was good, and pure, and I loved her. But you took her away."

Vic floundered for a response. Jordan cut in and said, "Mrs. Spencer, that's not fair. You know he wasn't happy."

"*He* wasn't happy? *He* wasn't here. Victoria was. But *he* had to ruin that."

"I don't know what you think was ruined, mom. I had a miserable childhood. We weren't the loving family you have stuck in your head. We didn't click. You always knew some-thing was wrong. I wasn't supposed to be your daughter. Maybe if you could accept it we could salvage what time we have left."

She shook her head. "Lies. The devil has filled your head full of lies and you don't remember all the wonderful things that happened."

"The wonderful things? The *wonderful*—" Vic started laughing. After a moment he said, "Wonderful like when dad left and you told me he died? I didn't see him again until his real funeral twenty years later."

"Your father was sick," Gloria spat.

"Mom, he was gay."

Gloria scowled. "I didn't want you to be like him."

"Being like him would be a blessing. He was happy. He met a good man and had a happy life. A life I was deprived of being a part of."

Jordan put his hand on Vic's arm. "We should go. This isn't helping."

"No!" Gloria said, her eyes bulging. "Don't go."

Keelan sat forward. Her eyes darted around the room. After a few seconds, she jumped up, swearing. "The bitch is stalling, waiting for the police to get here."

Vic leaned his head against the back of the sofa and exhaled. "Mom, tell me you didn't. Tell me you're not that shitty of a person."

Gloria pressed her lips into a thin line. "What else could I do? I find out my daughter is a murderer. I will not abide such behavior."

"A murderer?" Jordan asked.

Her cold eyes turned to him. "They told me what you did to that poor family. Killing those people right in front of their son? It's appalling."

"We didn't do that. Mom, you have to believe me."

"How can I?" she asked, shaking her head. "I don't know you."

Jordan pulled on Vic's sleeve. "Come on, man. We gotta go."

They stood and headed toward the front door. Gloria watched them go, making no move to stop them. At the door, Vic turned back for one last look at his mother. With a voice barely more than a whisper he said, "I love you, even though you don't deserve it," and closed the door for the last time.

———

THEY SPRINTED DOWN THE HALL TOWARD THE BACK EXIT, KEELAN in the lead. She slammed against the door and hurled herself outside into the evening light.

The rain had stopped.

McCoy stood ahead of them, his gun pointed at Keelan as she emerged from the apartment building. He said, "They'll be here any minute. Now that we know the rain is safe…"

"And they sent you to cut us off?" Vic asked. "Why, because they know you'll shoot innocent people?"

McCoy winced. "What happened at the restaurant—it was an accident. I never meant to hurt anyone."

"And now?" Jordan asked.

McCoy took a deep breath as if steadying his resolve. He lowered his gun and said, "Now I'm here to try to make it right. I can get you outta here."

Keelan chuckled. "Are you crazy? We can't trust a cop."

"I think we can," Jordan said, his eyes never leaving McCoy. "He's starting to see the truth."

McCoy swallowed. "The woman, Zoya, she told me what you said about the water. She told me not to let her boy drink it."

"Why would she tell you that?" Vic asked.

"I don't know."

Vic frowned. "What happened to Zoya?"

McCoy closed his eyes. When he spoke, he sounded as if he was choking on each word. "Dead. Killed in custody. They said she tried to run, but—"

"But she didn't," Jordan finished.

McCoy shook his head.

Vic cursed. He gestured toward McCoy and said, "We can't trust this guy."

"Whether you trust me or not, you still need to go. We've got about two minutes before the place is swarming with police."

"You radioed it in, didn't you?" Keelan asked.

He nodded. "I had to. But I waited until you were leaving your mother's apartment."

Keelan turned her back to him, putting her body between McCoy and the others. She whispered, "I can get us to the Crumbs. We can hole up there for the night until things die down."

"I like that plan better than the idea of going with a cop," Vic agreed.

Jordan shook his head. "They'll be onto that by now. We can't risk bringing more trouble to the Crumbs. They have it bad enough as is."

"You really think this guy is going to help us? He'll turn us in the first chance he gets," Vic said.

"Maybe," Jordan said with a shrug. "But I don't think so. And right now he's the best chance we've got."

Keelan put her hands on her hips and dropped her head. She stepped aside and let Jordan pass, moving closer to McCoy. Jordan said, "We've made a decision."

"First, I have something for you," McCoy said. He reached into his jacket, slowly withdrawing his hand. He held Reeva's journal toward Jordan. "I stole it when Deke wasn't looking."

Jordan chuckled. He turned to the others, who both

nodded their approval. Jordan gestured forward and said, "All right, McCoy. Lead the way."

———

THEY LEFT THE CITY CENTER AND MADE THEIR WAY TOWARD THE perimeter fence. Guards were stationed at regular intervals, keeping the healthy safe inside and the plague carriers out. Their guns gleamed in the spotlights swiveling across the area.

Jordan and his friends could see the plague tents growing larger as they neared the fence, tension building in each of them as they approached.

McCoy had led them through back alleys, listening to his radio before each move. Finally they were at the last block before the perimeter. If they went to end of the block, they'd be in the gap: one hundred feet of empty space between safety and the perimeter. No one was permitted in the gap without hazard gear unless they wanted to be shot.

"He's led us between a rock and a hard place," Vic said. "Cops behind, guards ahead."

McCoy waved his hand, shushing Vic. He listened to his radio another moment before a small smile turned up the corners of his lips. He looked up at Jordan and said, "Right on time."

A truck pulled around the block in front of them. There was a flashing light, but not sirens.

"A plague truck?" Vic asked. "That's your plan?"

McCoy nodded. "No one will look for you there."

"I'm not getting on a fucking plague truck," Vic said, backing away.

Jordan looked up at the sky, a broad grin on his face. "It's a lie. Everything is a lie."

Keelan asked, "What are you talking about?"

"The water, the rain, the plague. It's meant to keep us docile, maintained. We're prisoners here without realizing it."

"Jordan, there's no way to know that for sure," Vic said.

"It's just like the rain," Jordan said. "The plague isn't real. They're just reacting to the poisoned water."

McCoy nodded. "I think so, too. I don't know for sure, but it makes sense."

When the drivers got out and wheeled their carts to the building across the street, Jordan, Vic, and Keelan climbed into the back of the truck. There were bodies stacked inside— some were already dead.

McCoy shut one of the doors on the back of the truck. Before he closed the other, Jordan put his hand on his shoulder. "Thank you."

"I'm sorry I couldn't do more," McCoy said, shaking his head. "For you, for Zoya."

Jordan said, "You still can. From the inside. This thing isn't over."

"No," McCoy agreed. "It's just beginning."

CHAPTER 6

he truck made two more stops as they lay there in the dark, too fearful to speak, or move, or breathe. Their bodies were veiled among the sick and the dead. Jordan peeked out from behind a large man with clammy skin; he was still alive, but his breathing was shallow and his glassy eyes were unseeing.

The smooth pavement turned to gravel as the truck turned toward the perimeter fence protecting the city from the plague area. The rough road jostled them. A dead man's arm fell near Vic's mouth as he curled under a gurney. Jordan saw Vic's face pale, his sharp intake of breath, the slump of his shoulders; he was on the edge of losing it.

"Calm down," Jordan whispered. His voice was so soft to his own ears, he wondered if Vic could've heard him.

But he did. Jordan saw him close his eyes and nod, slinking as far away as he could from the fallen arm.

Jordan glanced to Keelan. She was slumped over, sprawled across a woman's lap. The woman could be dead or alive—Jordan couldn't tell—but either way, Keelan had positioned herself as if it didn't matter. She belonged there, among the sick and dying. Anyone who saw her wouldn't question it.

As he stared at her, the truck came to a sudden stop. He could hear voices at the front but couldn't make out the words. A barked command cut through the night. The doors were thrown open and flashlights shone into the truck, scanning the prone bodies.

Jordan pressed his chest against the fat man's belly. They were face-to-face, mere inches from one another. The smell of the dying man made it hard for Jordan to breathe; his mouth parted slightly, drawing in air as best he could. His stomach roiled as the taste of menthol and rot hit the back of his throat.

He surveyed the man, looking for any sign of decay but seeing nothing. His fleshy arm draped across Jordan in a protective embrace. Jordan's breath caught in his throat as he looked up into cloudy blue eyes. The man still looked on as if he couldn't see Jordan, but his lips turned up in the faintest of smiles. He whispered, "Paolo."

A relative, maybe? A lover? An ache filled Jordan's chest as he thought about all the bodies in all the plague trucks tonight, in all the trucks past, and those still to come. Every person sent to the plague zone had a Paolo, had a Reeva—each had been robbed of the chance to see their loves again.

The light shining on the man's cheek drew Jordan's attention. They were looking at him. Seconds passed, ticking by as Jordan stared at the glint of light, knowing in his heart that he was caught. Maybe if he gave himself up they wouldn't notice Keelan and Vic.

Just before he moved to surrender he heard someone outside the truck yell, "All clear. Let 'em through."

The door closed and a moment later the truck began moving again. They rode in silence for several minutes, longer than Jordan expected, before the truck stopped again. The doors opened and figures in HAZMAT suits began pulling the bodies out.

He felt a hand grab his ankle and pull. It took every ounce of restraint he had not to struggle. He closed his eyes and let them pull him from the truck. At the edge of the truck, someone checked his pulse. "Alive," a voice said. They carried him to the side of the truck and put him on the ground in a row with seven other bodies.

Jordan pressed his hands against the ground, the dirt creeping between his fingers. His brain flitted from one idea to the next, searching for a way to escape. Moments later, Keelan and Vic were with him, lined along the ground waiting for whatever came next.

"We have to get out of here," Jordan whispered.

"No," Keelan said. "If we go, they'll notice. We need to wait."

"Wait for what?" Vic asked.

"Don't worry. I'll signal my people," she said.

"How?" Jordan asked.

She shushed him as another body was brought toward them. After the suits were back at the truck, Vic said, "I can't just wait. I have to get out of here."

Keelan hissed, "Stop. I'll handle this."

But Jordan knew he couldn't. He'd seen that look on Vic's face before over the years. It always ended badly.

Vic lifted his head, his eyes scanning the truck for movement. When he saw no one, he jumped up and started running.

Keelan moved as if to go after him, but Jordan grabbed her wrist and pulled her back down. "No. We have to get to your contact."

"But Vic—"

"There's no stopping him now," Jordan said, resigned.

"He'll get himself killed."

"So will we if we try to stop him. Trust me. I know Vic. There's nothing to be done."

Keelan nodded, settling her head back into the dirt. Jordan took a deep breath and stared up into the sky. The haze of the city was fainter here and for a moment he almost thought he could see the stars. He couldn't, of course, and he knew no one had seen stars for years, but the thought of them still filled Jordan with curiosity and a sense of wonder, just as it had when he was a child.

Jordan's grandmother had taught him about the stars he couldn't see. She'd studied them, devoted her life to them, only to watch them disappear as perma-clouds blocked the sky. Jordan saw the way she'd look up at night, praying for a glimpse of one before her breath stopped. There was a deep longing in her eyes for something that had been lost to her, and it was only now as he searched the sky, his thoughts flitting to Reeva, that he understood.

The crunch of gravel pulled Jordan's attention from the stars, but to his credit he didn't move his head toward the approaching figures. The suits put another body at the end of the row. One of them pointed to the empty spot where Vic had been. "Hey Lem, wasn't there another one over here?"

"I dunno," Lem said. "Prolly spaced 'em out too far. It's not like one of these sickos could run away."

"Yeh, I guess," not-Lem said.

They trudged back toward the truck. After a moment, the engine sputtered to life and the truck pulled away. Jordan breathed a sigh of relief as he watched the truck grow smaller in the distance. He whispered, "I thought we were in trouble."

"Not yet," Keelan whispered back. "We'll wait here until they water us, then head out before the nurses get here."

"Water?" Jordan asked. The word caught in his throat, strangling him.

She sighed, and when she spoke it was as if she were explaining something to a child. "Don't drink it, obviously. When they put it to your mouth, let it dribble down your cheek."

"Won't that be suspicious?"

"These people are dying, Jordan. Most of them can't drink on their own already."

They waited.

It felt like hours, but Jordan was certain it wasn't more than thirty minutes. The waterers came as Keelan said they would. Moving down the line, the tall one carried a bucket while the other dipped a ladle and pressed it against the lips of the sick.

They seemed to be moving toward Jordan quickly, until they reached the woman three spaces down. The short waterer said, "She's not drinking. Hold her mouth open." The tall suit held the woman's mouth open, coaxing water down her throat.

Jordan felt Keelan's hand slide onto his arm. This wasn't part of the plan. He glanced at her from the corner of his eye, expecting to see terror on her face, but instead the corners of her lips were turned up in a smile. She mouthed, "Kill them."

Jordan's eyes bulged. She had to be joking. There was no way he could do it. He mouthed back, "I can't."

"You have to."

Jordan eyed the suits. They were two bodies away from him, tipping water into the mouth of a boy, ten years old, maybe eleven. Was his family mourning him tonight? Or were they already dead? Jordan clenched his fingers in the dirt as anger coursed through him. He heard the pounding in his ears, felt his blood boiling at the thought of what that child had lost.

They were watering the woman beside Jordan now. The short one was shaking their head, and Jordan's ears picked up the fragments of words spoken through their thick plastic helmets. "...just awful. I wish there was more we could do for them."

And Jordan knew then he couldn't hurt these people. They were bystanders, workers trying to survive however they could. They had nothing to do with the water or the sickness. Hell, they'd probably lost people of their own, not realizing the drink they provided was the nail in the coffin for some of the sick.

He unclenched his fists, closed his eyes, and waited for the water to come.

And waited.

When the water didn't come, Jordan eased his eyes open. The empty expanse of perma-clouds filled his view. He lifted his head. In the gravel by his feet, one of the suits, the short one, was on the ground. Thick, dark liquid pooled around the body, oozing onto Jordan's boot. Jordan shuddered. He pulled his foot back, wiping the blood in the grass.

He looked to Keelan, but her spot on the ground was empty. Of course it was. She'd done what he couldn't. She was probably finishing off the second suit right now.

Jordan stood and wiped the dirt from his pants. He looked around for Keelan but couldn't see past the tents lined up as far as his eyes could see. He spun around, unsure where to go. Keelan was his way to safety, his way to Reeva. Jordan ran his fingers through his hair, sighing, wondering if he should lie down and wait for her to return.

No, that was a foolish thought. She'd told him others would come once they'd been watered. With one of the suits bleeding on the ground, there was no way the new arrivers would let the empty spots on the ground go unnoticed.

A click echoed behind him in the quiet. A gun. The safety off. He put his shaking hands in the air and slowly turned to face the person behind him.

"Why the fuck do you have your hands in the air?" Keelan asked.

Jordan looked at the weapon in her hand and stammered, "I heard the gun and just—"

"Never mind," she said, waving her free hand dismissively. "We gotta go."

Jordan saw a tall figure running toward them. The other

waterer. He pointed, and Keelan spun toward the approaching suit, aiming her gun at their head. A second later she lowered the gun and turned back to him with a broad smile.

The suit stopped in front of them, removing their helmet. They were spindly, with thick brown hair coifed above the shaved sides of their head. Blood painted the front of their gear. So it wasn't Keelan who killed the other waterer.

"This is the guy I told you about," Keelan said, motioning to Jordan.

The suit held their hand out and said, "Good to meet you. I'm Moss."

Jordan shook their hand, surprised at the ease with which they smiled in such a situation. It made Jordan uneasy. He frowned and said, "Jordan."

"Enough with the pleasantries," Keelan said. "We need to get out of here before the next group arrives."

"Don't worry, babe. You're with me now," Moss said, throwing their arm around her shoulders.

Keelan smacked at their stomach, letting her hand linger there. She fought against a grin as she said, "You're more trouble than you're worth."

Moss donned a hurt expression, but couldn't hold it long. They leaned their forehead against Keelan's and said, "You like my kind of trouble."

"You bet your ass I do," she growled back. Keelan grabbed Moss's shirt and pulled their face to hers. She pressed her lips against theirs ferociously.

Jordan felt his cheeks flush. He turned his back to them, offering what little privacy he could. A bit later—Jordan wasn't sure how long he stood in awkward anticipation— they parted and moved to leave. He followed Keelan and Moss through the camp, weaving in and out of tents as they left the faint lights of the city at their back.

The plague tents were vast, spreading for miles in every

direction. Jordan had never before realized how many there were. He'd stared at them from his apartment window, or seen glimpses of them as he walked to the factory each morning, but he'd never given consideration to how many there were.

As they moved farther in, the odor hit Jordan like a brick. He hasn't noticed it from the edges of the camp, but now it was so thick in the air he could almost see the stench.

"Breathe through your mouth," Keelan said.

Jordan did, regretting it immediately. "I can taste it."

Moss handed him a small white disc. "Put this in your mouth. It'll help."

Jordan did as Moss said, thankful for the minty flavor that now covered his tongue.

They passed a tent with the flap up. Four beds were lined up side by side, but the bodies covering them overflowed from one bed to another, to the floor around, to limbs stretching out under the edges of the tent. Jordan felt his stomach flip. He hadn't noticed the arms and legs reaching for him from the tents before, but now he saw them everywhere he went, every turn they made. This wasn't a place to save those with the plague; this was a morgue.

The tents stopped abruptly. Massive spotlights shone ahead, lighting up the darkness beyond. Jordan hesitated just past the last row, staring at the trees a hundred feet ahead. They stretched out in either direction, a natural barrier. Jordan had never seen trees, at least, not like these. In the city there were trees on some corners, and a small park near the center of town where Reeva had liked to walk when they were newlyweds. But that was when they were whole—before the water illness, before the affair, even before the miscarriage that drove a wedge between them.

And those trees at the park were small, manicured, precise. Not like the hulking things that stood before him.

These trees were wild; vines hung from them in sweeping strands, coloring the horizon a rich swathe of green.

"Let's go," Keelan said.

"Give him a minute," Moss said with their easy smile. "Don't you remember the first time you saw it?"

Keelan looked from Jordan to the trees. She sighed, and when she spoke again her voice was tinged with sadness. "It's overwhelming. Beauty like you've never seen before. And it feels like the magic in storybooks is suddenly real."

Jordan nodded, swallowing the lump in his throat. "Yes. That."

She stepped toward him and put her small hand on his arm. "I know. I'm sorry I can't let you appreciate it a little longer, but we need to move. They've definitely realized we're gone by now and we need to get to cover before they find us in the gap."

"Right," Jordan said. He turned, looking back to the tents, his thoughts turning to Vic. He wouldn't be able to find them once they left the plague zone. If he was even still alive to find them. He scrubbed a hand over the stubble of his beard, trying to wipe away the worry.

Keelan seemed to read his thoughts. She turned to Moss and said, "Can you get someone to find his friend?"

"Already on it," Moss said. "Spades went after him when we saw him run."

Jordan took a deep breath, allowing himself a moment of relief. If they'd already sent someone, Vic would be fine. They could bring him into the woods with them and everything would be fine. He looked down into Keelan's fierce green eyes and forced himself to smile. "Let's go."

They set off across the empty expanse toward the trees.

CHAPTER 7

Jordan shivered as he trailed behind Keelan and Moss, his thoughts as dark as the woods around them. His flashlight cut a path of light in front of him, but the thick trees kept him from seeing more than a few feet ahead.

After an hour of keeping a brutal pace they stopped to rest near an outcropping of rocks. Moss passed around a canteen. Jordan eyed it warily until Keelan said, "Don't worry. This is clean water from camp. It won't hurt you."

He pressed the container to his lips, swallowing greedily.

"Slow down," Moss said. "You'll make yourself sick."

Jordan lowered the water and nodded. He wiped his sleeve against his mouth and handed the canteen back to Moss. "Thanks."

They nodded, smiling their strange, unbreakable smile. "We'll be at camp by dawn if we keep pushing. You doing okay?"

"I'm good," he said. Jordan wasn't as young as Keelan and Moss, but he wasn't some old fogey either. Years of working the factory line had kept him in shape, even if he was a little soft around the middle.

They pressed on, trudging through the woods. The walk was longer than he expected, and with the past few days of little sleep and less food and water, his body was more tired than it had ever been. Still, every time his thoughts turned to complaints, he chided himself. Of course it was a long walk—they had to be far enough away to stay hidden. And at the end of this walk, he'd see Reeva. That was all that really mattered.

Just when Jordan thought he couldn't take another step, they emerged from the woods into a small clearing. Past the clearing was a makeshift wall built from wood, rocks, and scraps of metal—anything that could be carried by human hands. Behind the wall, broken buildings stood tall with trees growing through them. Ivy clung to the sides of the structures in thick strands.

Jordan realized that while he stared ahead, Keelan and Moss had continued walking. He jogged to catch up though his eyes never left the concrete jungle ahead of him. When they reached the perimeter, a small door opened and three armed guards emerged. The two in the lead parted, their guns trained on Jordan.

The third guard walked toward Moss. He reached forward, gripped Moss's forearm, and said, "'Bout time you got back."

Moss smiled. "I missed you, too."

The guard moved to Keelan and shook her hand. "Welcome back. You're in for it."

"I know," she said. "But I got the goods."

He nodded and stepped to Jordan. "And who are you?"

"Jordan Adler."

"Adler?" the man said, raising one eyebrow.

"Eric, this is Reeva's husband," Keelan said. "And this is Moss's brother, Eric."

A small smile spread across Eric's face. "You are not what I was expecting."

"What does that mean?" Jordan asked.

"Nothing, man," Eric said. "I've heard Reeva talk about

you a few times and I thought you'd be, I don't know, bigger."

"Bigger?"

Eric shrugged. "Anyway, it's good to meet you. Let's head into camp and find the boss."

Bigger? Jordan thought. What exactly had Reeva been saying about him?

They walked through the gates, the other two guards closing it behind them. Eric led them down the main street. It was cracked, with weeds and flowers growing through it, but Jordan could see it had once been wide enough for several cars to drive abreast.

"Why is the street so wide?" he asked Keelan as she walked beside him.

"Dunno," she said. "Maybe their vehicles were bigger."

"There were a lot more of them. More people, more cars," Moss said.

"What happened to them?"

Keelan eyed him, her expression drifting between confusion and exasperation. "You really don't know?" Jordan shook his head and she continued. "Most people left, moved south to Detroit because of the war, but there were survivors who stuck it out. When it came time to rebuild, they left this place for nature to reclaim and built New Flint."

"That doesn't make sense," Jordan said. "Our city has been there forever. Since before the Water War that was what, seventy-five years ago? We stayed out of it and took care of ourselves."

"After everything you've learned, how can you recite that old story as if you believe it? It's called *New* Flint for a reason," she asked.

Jordan stammered for a moment before saying, "I guess I didn't give it much thought."

A voice behind them said, "He doesn't know how deep the lies run."

Jordan turned, his heart stuck in his throat. Reeva stood in the middle of the street. Her black curls were pulled up on her head. Her face was an acorn, both in shape and shade, and Jordan marveled at the way her skin seemed to glow from some inward light. The corner of Reeva's lips was quirked up in a smile—her shy smile—revealing the dimple on her left cheek.

"Hi," he said, raising his hand.

She laughed at him, the awkward way he greeted her, the way he didn't know how to talk to his own wife after only a couple months of being apart. But her laugh wasn't derisive; no, her laugh was full of love. It was the laugh of someone who expected nothing else, who loved him for exactly who he was.

At least, that's the laugh he heard.

"What are you doing here?" she asked.

Jordan wasn't sure why the question bothered him so much. Maybe it was the way it accused him of doing something wrong, the way it relayed that she wasn't happy to see him. What could he say? The obvious answer was that she was here and he belonged at her side, but he wasn't sure she wanted to hear that. There was also that pesky business with the police and the journal and the truth of the water. But those things seemed so small in comparison with his need to be where she was.

"I brought him," Keelan said, stepping forward. "I went for your journal and found him in trouble, so I helped him get away."

Reeva nodded. She took a step forward and placed her hand against his cheek. "I'm glad you're okay."

Jordan gritted his teeth as he stared into the amber eyes he knew so well. There was a flare of anger in his chest, sudden and fierce, and he wanted to scream at her almost as much as he wanted to pull her against him, to entangle their bodies in an embrace. She'd left him to think she was dead, running off with these strangers instead of telling him what was happening. He could've been next to get sick from the water and she would've never known.

He moved his face, letting her hand fall away. The sight of her was too much. Instead he stared at the clothesline across the street, garments drying between two broken buildings. He said, "Yeah. Glad to see you're well, too."

The seconds ticked by in uncomfortable silence. Eric finally said, "We're taking him to Lady Q for the official welcome. You can come if you want."

Reeva shook her head. "Probably better if I don't."

"She's not good at sticking around. Better you know it early than find out ten years in," Jordan said.

He didn't know where the words came from, didn't know he felt that way. Only a few minutes ago he'd wanted to take her in his arms and never let go. But now, standing in front of her, the only thing he could find in his heart was anger, hurt.

She squinted her eyes, her fists balling at her sides. "I was doing what I thought was best for you."

"Oh, come on," Jordan said, rolling his eyes. "You didn't give two shits about what happened to me or you never would've left like you did."

"You act like I had a choice in all this."

"There's always a choice, Ree. Always."

"And I chose to protect you."

"By letting me think the plague workers came for you? By letting me think you were dead?" He spun away from her, taking a deep breath and expelling it forcefully. He looked at Keelan and the others watching them and said, "Can you give us a minute?"

They nodded in unison and moved off. Jordan turned back to her, his voice thin when he asked, "Why would it be better for me to think you were dead?"

"It gave you a chance to move on, without being caught up in all this," she said, waving her hands around to indicate the dilapidated city around them. "But you couldn't let it go, could you? You've never been able to let things go."

Jordan huffed. "No, I couldn't let it go. Not you. Not the miscarriage. Not the affair with my best fucking friend. Never, ever you. Especially not after I found this." Jordan pulled Reeva's journal from the back of his jeans and waved it in front of her.

"You were never supposed to see that," she said, her voice cracking.

"Well I did. Every last word." He tossed the journal on the pavement in front of her feet. "I'm so fucking sorry for caring about you."

Jordan turned and started away from her. The others were standing stock-still, but they jumped into motion after he passed them. Eric jogged ahead to lead the way, while Keelan and Moss brought up the rear. None dared speak of what had happened, or if they did, Jordan couldn't hear them over the screaming in his head as he replayed the conversation over and over and over.

———

THEY STOPPED IN FRONT OF A TALL GRAY BUILDING WITH HALF the roof caved in. Eric led them up the steps and into the foyer. Signs of the building's former glory were everywhere: cracked marble floors, thick columns crumbled and pitted with holes, and a crystal chandelier still managing to cling to the ceiling with only a few pieces missing.

"What is this place?" Jordan asked. His voice echoed from the vaulted ceilings, eerie in the dim space.

"Used to be some sort of government building, we think," Moss said. "Now it belongs to Lady Q."

"You say the name like I should know who it is."

"You should," a voice said, forceful, final.

A petite woman approached them, decked out in a leather

jumpsuit. Her black and silver hair was pulled back into a ponytail, swishing behind her head as she walked. Jordan sized her up as she stopped in front of him. She was older than him, late forties maybe, pretty, with almond-shaped eyes and pale pink lips. A small black mole dotted her temple by her eyebrow, above the barely visible scar that traced her cheekbone.

"How long do you plan to stare at me?" she asked.

Jordan started. He opened his mouth to apologize, but decided against it. He wasn't sure who she was, Lady Q or someone else, but something about her said she wouldn't appreciate any show of weakness. Instead he asked, "Who the hell are you?"

Her glare hardened, but her mouth curved into an amused smile. She held her arms wide and said, "I'm the one you came to see, smartass. I decide your fate."

"Shit," he muttered.

Keelan stepped up beside him and bowed her head. "I'm sorry, Lady Q. I should've prepared him before meeting you."

Lady Q folded her arms across her chest as she turned her scowl to Keelan. "You think you're the best ambassador for him?"

Keelan winced. "I know what I did was wrong."

"You disobeyed my explicit instructions, Keelan."

"I know," Keelan said. "But I also know it was important to get the journal before the police found it. And I did."

"Sure, you did, but you also left a mess to clean up and a trail that leads directly back to us."

Keelan shook her head. "No, everything is settled. We had some trouble at the beginning but—"

"Stop," Lady Q interrupted. "Let's retrace your steps, shall we? You murdered a police officer, before leading outsiders through the Crumbs, where we do business. You let yourself be seen by numerous police officers, compromising yourself for any future missions. You let one of those cops go when you had a chance to eliminate him. And then you bring a new mouth to feed, complicating things with one of our current members. Did I miss anything?"

"No," Keelan said, her voice less than a whisper.

"I didn't think so."

"How did you know all that?" Jordan asked.

Her eyes turned to him. "That's none of your concern."

"It is, actually. Because if you know that much about what happened, why didn't you step in to help us? And what do you know about about my friend and his whereabouts? Someone was supposed to go look for him."

Lady Q raked her tongue across her teeth. Without taking her eyes off him, she said, "Leave us," and the others scurried from the foyer like roaches running from the light. She motioned with her head for him to follow, then turned and walked through a door along the wall.

Jordan followed her through a maze of rooms. Shattered windows let the cold in, each gust of wind sending dust motes wandering through the air to settle on fragmented bits of furniture and the broken shelves that lined the wall.

Finally she stopped in a room that appeared whole. The window was intact and a fire roared in the fireplace. All signs of destruction that filled the other areas had been removed, wiped clean, leaving gleaming hard wood and polished glass reclaimed from the nature it had been given over to.

Lady Q poured herself a drink from a crystal decanter before reclining on a settee near the fireplace. Jordan licked his lips, longing for a drink after their long walk, but refusing to ask. He walked to a chair across from her, removed the books stacked there, and sat down. He watched her, waiting for her to speak, though her eyes were focused on the dancing fire.

After several minutes Jordan stood and said, "I've got shit to do, lady. I'll show myself out."

"You aren't a patient person, are you Mr. Adler?"

He stared down at her. "No, not anymore. Seems like the time for waiting is over."

She smiled. "Please. Sit. We have much to discuss. You deserve to know how you ended up here, at the very least."

"A failing marriage and a dash of bad luck," Jordan said. "I don't imagine you have much more to add to that."

But Jordan sat down, prepared to bolt out if there was nothing to be gained from the conversation. But Lady Q was true to her word, and with a deep breath she spoke, saying, "It all comes back to the war we've fought for nearly eighty years."

Jordan rolled his eyes. "That's preposterous. We haven't had a war since my grandmother was a child."

She sighed. "If you're going to hear this, you need to keep your mind open. Forget the lies you've been taught and just listen. Can you do that or am I wasting my breath?"

"I can listen. You've gotta understand though, this is new. It isn't easy to take in. And honestly, you've given me no reason to trust you so far."

"That's fair," she said. "I've been here all my life, grew up with parents in the rebellion. You grew up in the false city, safe. You didn't know they were lying to you. That's one thing I can guarantee I won't do. I may be a lot of things, Mr. Adler, but I'm no liar."

Jordan nodded and said, "If we're going to be allies, we can start with you calling me Jordan."

She paused for a moment, squinting at him, before saying, "Quincy. But I'm Lady Q when the others are present."

"Okay Quincy, tell me the truth. All of it."

"Like I said, we've been at war. Or more accurately, we lost the war and have been trying to fix things since. You at least know about the Water War, right?"

"Of course. The water was undrinkable. People were going to war for clean drinking water, looting, fighting, killing. Went on for nearly a year before the federal government finally stepped in and got things straightened out."

"That's the story they tell. But the truth is they used the war as an excuse to implement a new program to manage the citizens. They gave us drinkable water that was drugged to make the residents docile. Once they saw it worked, they moved on to other cities."

"Wait, you're saying the government is *definitely* poisoning people to make them easier to control? I mean, I thought it was possible, but part of me also thought I might be losing my mind."

"It's definitely happening. Control is how it started. And it went well for a while, but then people started getting sick. So they set up the plague zones and quarantined the cities as a cover for what they were doing. That made it even easier to keep control of people. They can't leave their assigned city because of a plague. Information doesn't get passed around as much, since the government took control of the phones and internet."

"I don't know," Jordan said, shaking his head. "Seems like people would notice something like that."

"People notice what's in their face at the moment. Once that moment is gone, they move on to whatever holds their fleeting attention next."

"But people talk. They couldn't stop that."

"Couldn't they? Didn't they shut up that nice Russian couple you met?"

"How do you know about them? That happened before Keelan was with us."

Quincy raised a brow. "And you think she's my only operative in the city?"

"I hadn't really considered—"

"Don't worry," she interrupted. "We retrieved the little boy, Dimitri. He'll be well in a week or so."

"I'm glad. He didn't deserve to be sick."

"None of them do, Jordan. But the population can be managed and kept under the government's thumb simply by filling them full of drugs."

Jordan sat in silence, staring at the fire. Quincy's words rang of truth. He could see she wasn't lying, but there was still something about the whole thing that made him uneasy. There was something she wasn't telling him, a secret she wanted to keep.

"Tell me about your other operative."

Quincy pursed her lips. "I can't do that. For their safety, of course."

"Do you consider me a threat?"

"Everyone who isn't one of us is a threat."

And there it was. "And what do you do with threats, Quincy? Say for example, I ran away."

"You would be dealt with."

"What if you couldn't catch me? What if I got away?"

"No one gets away."

"Vic did," he said.

She held her breath a second too long. "So he did."

Jordan huffed as it all clicked into place. "Because he's already yours, isn't he?"

Lady Q smiled. "You're far cleverer than I expected. Reeva thought you'd be easy to deal with. But there's more to you than she realizes."

"Reeva hasn't known me for a long time. I just didn't realize how far we'd drifted until now."

"You know about her and Vic?"

Jordan nodded. "He was there for her when I wasn't. I was hurt, after the baby…" he trailed off. "But Vic, he was my best friend. So if he could help her through it, I wanted him to."

"But it was more than that."

"Yeah," he said, his mouth going dry. He coughed, cleared his throat. "Yeah, it was more. They had an affair. It was rough for a long time, but eventually I forgave them both. I stayed with Reeva. I stayed friends with Vic, at least, as much as I could."

"It didn't end, Jordan. You know that."

He ground his teeth together. He did know. He'd always known, somewhere in the back of his head. He'd just never wanted to admit it.

"I'm sorry," she said. "But I told you, I won't lie."

"You're willing to withhold the truth though."

"If my operatives can stay secret, obviously that's what I want," she said with a shrug.

"So you sent him to what? Kill me?" Jordan asked.

Quincy held a hand to her chest. "God no. We had no interest in you. You'd still be blissfully ignorant if you hadn't read Reeva's journal. But once you told Vic what you knew about the water, we couldn't have you running around town blabbing about it."

"Why not? Seems like that's what you'd want to help stop what they're doing."

She shook her head. "No one is going to believe some crazy guy who just lost his wife to the plague. The cops would've taken you into custody and you'd be dead by now."

"Maybe that's what should've happened," he said, bitterness seeping into his words.

"Maybe," she said. "Probably would've been easier. But Reeva and Vic love you, even if that's hard to see."

Jordan laughed, a sour, joyless sound. "They *love* me? Then why did they betray me?"

With a shrug she said, "That's not something I can answer."

"Of course not."

"I can tell you about our cause, I can invite you to be part of something bigger than yourself, but I can't answer why the heart wants what it wants."

Jordan jumped to his feet. "I need some air."

Quincy picked up a small silver bell on the table beside the settee and rang it once. Seconds later a man was at the door, hand on the gun at his hip. "Lady Q?" he asked.

"This gentleman is my personal guest. Take him to guestroom three and make sure he has anything he needs. He is free to walk about as he wishes, but if he tries to leave the camp, kill him."

"Yes, Lady," the man said.

He led Jordan from Quincy's receiving room to the other side of the complex, down a white hallway trimmed in dirt and scorch marks. He opened a door off the hallway and took Jordan inside. It wasn't elegant like Quincy's room, but it was clean and there was a bed. Jordan's head pounded as he realized how long it had been since he'd slept. He walked over and sat down, not even realizing the guard had left.

Jordan rolled to the middle of the bed. He'd spent ten years sleeping on the left because Reeva liked to be on the side away from the window. Even when she'd been missing, presumed dead, he slept facing the window, letting the light coming in wake him every morning.

He rolled over once more, faced the window, and fell asleep.

CHAPTER 8

t was evening when he woke. The golden clouds behind the trees were beautiful and Jordan lay there several minutes marveling at how lovely the world could be. He felt surprised at the thought, not because it wasn't true, or because so many bad things had happened, but because he'd never had the thought before. Sure, he'd seen beautiful things and known beautiful people, but the world has always seemed a little too cold for his taste.

But this was a new world. A world without lies built around him, walling him into a life that wasn't true. This was a life without Reeva.

Jordan rolled off the bed and walked to the door. He wandered down the dirty hall, through the foyer, and out into the camp. The smell of meat and the sound of laughter pulled him down the street. He paid careful attention to the route he took, trying to make sure he could get back on his own if he needed to. Jordan watched for signs of how many people lived here, but it was impossible to tell with so many buildings in shambles, side-by-side, all looking the same.

Around a squat building with flaking blue paint, he found a group of people milling about around a bonfire. They were talking, laughing, living—something Jordan hadn't done for a long time. He saw a ball of ruby-red hair bounding toward him. Keelan. For a moment he thought she was going to hug him, but she stopped instead, hesitating.

"Hey," she said, nodding her head.

He forced a smile. "Hey."

"I wasn't sure what Lady Q would do with you."

"Me either," he said, rubbing at the stubble on his chin.

"But you're allowed to stay?"

"I guess," he shrugged. "She gave me a room and told me to look around."

Keelan blinked, surprised. "A room at her place? I've never known her to do that before."

"She's probably never had a guy show up to the rebellion to find out his wife wanted him to believe she was dead so she could be with his best friend, who also happens to be a rebellion spy."

"Yeah," she said, elongating the word as if it somehow sympathized with everything he'd just said. "That's a lotta shit to deal with at once."

"You pretended like you didn't know him."

"I don't, not really. I've seen him around the camp, but we've never been friends."

"But you knew he was with Reeva. And you knew what that would mean if I came here."

Keelan shrugged. "That part isn't my business. I got you out of the city because it was the right thing to do. It was either that or let you die."

"My wife and my best friend were willing to leave me."

"Just because you've got some assholes in your life doesn't mean I have to be one, too."

Jordan smiled. "Thank you. I don't know where I'd be if not for you."

"Yes, you do."

She was right. He knew what would've happened without her intervention. He bit his lip, thinking about poor Zoya and

Fedya. They were dead because they'd tried to help him. Dimitri would grow up without his parents, because they were kind. He swallowed hard, shook his head, and changed the subject. "Besides my shitty family situation, there's the whole 'lying government poisoning its citizens' bit. It's a little heavy."

She nodded. "I remember when they gave me the talk. But it was probably a little easier for me. Aunt Aysie was never a fan of the government, so I heard a lot of crazy stories growing up."

"Aunt Aysie? The woman in the Crumbs market?"

"The one and only."

"I thought she hated you," he said with a chuckle.

Keelan shrugged. "She's not happy with my line of work."

"Why not? Seems like working for rebels would suit her."

She winced, but Moss approached before she could answer. They laid their arm across Keelan's shoulders and smiled at Jordan. "Glad to see you made it out okay. Hungry?"

Jordan put his hand on his stomach, trying to disguise the rumble that answered. "Starving."

Moss led him past the bonfire where people congregated and over to a small fire with a heavy pot suspended above it. They handed him a bowl and spoon from a stack to the side of the small fire, ladling a steaming soup into Jordan's bowl. Moss directed him to a log seat while they walked back toward the bonfire with Keelan.

Jordan finished half the bowl before he thought to taste it. It was thick, buttery, with chunks of potatoes and meat he couldn't identify. It could use a little salt, but was otherwise pleasant. As he was finishing his dinner, Lady Q approached. She handed him a tall glass of water and sat beside him on the log.

"We get along, for the most part," she said, as if continuing a conversation from before. "The people here recognize the importance of our mission and can let other issues fall to the side."

"Good for them," Jordan said.

Quincy sighed. "So that leaves you. Do you think you can let it go?"

He turned his head toward her. "Could you?"

"I don't know," she said. After a minute she added, "I've never loved anyone."

Jordan turned toward the fire. With a sigh he said, "I don't know if I can let it go, Q. I'd love to give you a different answer, to pretend that I was fine with all this, but I can't do that."

"I wouldn't want you to anyway," she said. "I'd rather hear an ugly truth than a pretty lie."

He stood, offering his hand to help her stand. She stood, but didn't take it. He smiled, looked down at her, and said, "I'd like to stay. Even though I don't know how to deal with it all, I still want to be here. I can't go back knowing what I know."

She nodded. "Two weeks. That gives us both time to make sure this is the right fit."

"And if it isn't?"

She shrugged. "Let's just hope it is."

———

Two weeks came and went without Jordan seeing Quincy again. If he wasn't a good fit, no one bothered to tell him. He thought they would tell him, if they needed to; in fact, they told him everything else. Quincy had instilled a desire for truth in all of them and they weren't afraid to speak their minds.

Unfortunately, the desire to speak the truth had made its way into Reeva as well. She had found him at the bonfire the third night after he'd arrived.

"I want to talk to you," she said.

Jordan was mid-sip from the small bottle of whiskey Moss had given him. He swallowed the drink, relishing the burn down his throat. "Okay. Talk."

"I care about you, J. I always have."

He nodded. "I know, Ree."

"But things with Vic, well," she paused, looking off into the distance as a smile crossed her face before disappearing into her solemn expression again, "it's just different."

"Different. Sure. That clears everything up. Thanks so much," Jordan said, rolling his eyes.

She huffed. "It wasn't easy being in love with both of you."

Jordan coughed, caught off guard by her words. "Oh yeah? It sounds awful. I can't imagine how much I would hate it if two people were in love with me."

Reeva shook her head. "I'm talking about the ripping inside me every time I saw you, every time I saw him. The way my heart felt both full and empty simultaneously. I couldn't keep doing it, J. I had to choose."

"And you chose the one who wasn't your husband."

He stood and walked away, and despite the pain roiling inside him, he had no desire to look back.

———

SHE CORNERED HIM ON THREE MORE OCCASIONS, TRYING TO TELL him about her relationship with Vic, her complicated feelings for Jordan, and what made her leave when and how she did. Jordan went the other way now when he saw her coming, hoping to avoid the bile that rose in his throat every time she spoke to him.

Vic, meanwhile, was nowhere to be seen. Jordan had heard that he was fine, that he had returned to camp after his run through the plague tents, but he was gone soon after on another mission for Quincy. Jordan wondered, briefly, if Quincy had sent him on a mission as a favor to give him time to adjust to life with the rebels without the constant pain of seeing Vic and Reeva together. He dismissed the thought just as quickly; Quincy didn't seem like the sort to do anyone a favor without the promise of a tenfold return.

Days at the camp were much like his days in the city: up early, work until he was bone-tired, stumble home for a shower. But his evenings were a different story. They were rich with laughter, full of new friends and stories he'd never imagined, thick with the promise of a better future. It had been so long since he'd felt hope, he'd almost forgotten how intoxicating it could be.

After a month of living with the rebels, he got up one morning to find Quincy standing in his room by the window, her back to him.

Still staring outside she said, "Vic is back."

Jordan grunted. "I don't know what you want me to say."

"Speak the truth," she said. "How do you feel?"

He took a deep breath and closed his eyes. He'd been working with Moss to better access his truth, to learn to read his emotions with purity but without reaction. It had been strange at first, accessing the feelings he'd long kept buried, but soon he realized that was why Moss's smile had made him so uncomfortable. It was pure, a reflection of their freedom.

Vic would've thought the whole thing was a bunch of bullshit. Or maybe not. Turns out the man he'd known since he was a child wasn't exactly who Jordan thought he was.

"I don't know him. Not the real him."

"Explain," she said.

"I know the man he let me see. Or maybe the man I wanted to see. But he is someone else."

"Does that bother you?"

"Yes. I miss my friend."

"Did you ever wish he wouldn't come back?"

Jordan paused, pushed out his breath. "Yes. But I regret that thought. I'm glad he's safe."

"And if he were here, now, what would you say to him?"

"I understand."

"You understand why he had the affair? Why he betrayed you?" she asked.

"I understand why he fell in love with Reeva, why she fell in love with him. I loved them both. So I understand."

Quincy took a deep breath and asked, "Do you forgive him?"

"No," Jordan said, quicker than he meant to. "I don't know if I ever will. Understanding is the best I can do for now."

There was a moment of quiet. Jordan opened his eyes. She was gone.

———

JORDAN SKIPPED THE BONFIRE THAT NIGHT. THE THOUGHT OF seeing Vic and Reeva celebrating his return made Jordan ill. Instead he grabbed a canteen, a chunk of cheese, and a heel of bread and headed up to the Eagle's Nest.

The Nest was the tallest building in the broken city, allowing Jordan the best views of his new home. It was a quiet place. He often found himself retreating there when he was feeling out of sorts, or when Reeva tried to share her truths again.

He stared out into the night, tiny fires dancing in his vision as the people below prepared meals and enacted their evening rituals. There was lightning in the distance. Silver crashed through the perma-clouds, giving nanoseconds of brightness to the sky above. He couldn't hear the thunder yet, but the rain would come before the night was over, of that he was sure.

He wasn't afraid of the rain anymore. There wasn't much that still held power over him. And after he'd told the camp about running from the cops in a downpour, providing concrete proof that it really was just another lie from the government, the rebels didn't hide from it either. At least he'd been able to offer them that, though there wasn't much else he could do for them.

Jordan sat at the edge of the Nest until his food was gone and his canteen was empty. The fires below had faded to embers. He stood and made his way through the metal frame that was all that remained of the top floors. He climbed down into the belly of the building and headed for the stairwell.

He heard giggling echoing up from the stairs below. Jordan froze. He didn't want to disrupt someone's tryst, but he was too tired to climb back up and wait it out. With a sigh, he stepped into the stairwell and started down the steps. He jogged down, attempting to make enough noise as to not surprise the couple. As he rounded the stairs on the fourth floor, he saw them.

Vic and Reeva.

She was pressed against the wall, her head tilted back and her hand in Vic's hair as he knelt in front of her. She moaned and bucked against his tongue as her eyes came open.

"What the fuck?" she yelled.

Jordan swallowed the bile in his throat, pressing down the pain as he floundered for something to say, anything to explain why he was standing there, watching them. But there was no explanation.

Vic stood, crossing the distance between him and Jordan in two strides. He was inches from Jordan's face, spittle flying with each word as he asked, "Are you following us? What the hell is wrong with you?"

Jordan felt his face burn hot. He could smell Reeva in the tight corridor—her sweat, the salt on her skin. Vic reeked of her.

"I asked you a question," Vic said, jabbing his finger against Jordan's chest.

"You need to back the fuck off, Vic," Jordan said, his fists balled at his side. "I was coming down from the Nest. Trust me, *that* is the last thing I wanted to see."

Vic's face dropped, losing his anger. His eyes lost their fire, and Jordan saw something else staring back instead. Guilt? Shame?

Jordan shook his head. Let the fucker feel what he wanted. Jordan no longer cared. He pushed past Vic and continued down the stairs, his mind's eye burning with their entwined image.

———

JORDAN STUMBLED THROUGH THE PRE-DAWN LIGHT TOWARD THE mess. He was working the farm this week and he dare not be late or Mazzie would have him pulling weeds all morning. The smell of fried potatoes and onions smacked him in the gut as he walked through the door, reminding him of his meager dinner the night before.

There were only a handful of other people there so early—Vic was one of them. Jordan felt his body tense up and his hunger dissipate. He turned back toward the door, but stopped short when Mazzie stepped in front of him.

"Nope," she said, her toothless grin filling his vision. "You gotta get it over with."

"There's nothing to say," Jordan growled.

She sniffed, her lips puckering up until they almost touched her nose. "I'd bet there's at least a little to say to the person bedding your wife."

Jordan took a deep breath, holding it in as if trying to stop time. When he saw that Mazzie wasn't going to move, and he knew he wasn't going to try to make her, he released his breath and turned to face Vic.

Vic had crossed the room and was standing behind him. His dark hair was longer now, unbound around his shoulders. Jordan stared at it, wondering if he would've noticed if he'd still been seeing Vic every day.

"Can we talk?" Vic asked, his tone unusually soft.

Jordan gritted his teeth. He huffed and nodded toward an empty table by the window, away from the ears of the others. They sat across from each other, eyes searching the other one's, neither of them speaking. Jordan noticed a scar on Vic's top lip as he licked them nervously; he couldn't help the curiosity about how he got it. He imagined half a dozen dangerous scenarios where Vic was the brave hero, before finally settling on the image of Vic getting a nasty paper cut while bumbling through some mail. He knew it wasn't accurate, but it made him smile all the same.

Jordan's smile seemed to give Vic the encouragement he needed, and he smiled back. Vic said, "I'm sorry. You know, about last night."

Leaning back in his chair Jordan said, "You should be."

Vic's brow furrowed. "I'm talking about accusing you of following us. I was wrong for that."

"What about the part where you were tongue-fucking my wife? Were you wrong for that, too?"

Vic shot up, knocking his chair to the ground. "Stop calling her that. She hasn't been yours for a long time."

"She was until you stole her from me."

Reeva stepped up to their table, her rich eyes furious. "Let's get something straight right now: I'm not a possession or a prize for either of you assholes. I am with whom I choose to be with. But if you want to act like I'm some toy to fight over, believe me, I can do without you both."

She turned and stormed from the mess as they watched her in stunned silence. They looked back at each other, Jordan's brown eyes meeting Vic's baby blues. After a few seconds, they both smiled.

Vic said, "She knows who she is and she's not afraid to say so."

"That's why I loved her," Jordan said.

"Me, too," Vic agreed.

Jordan sighed. "Look, I'm still hurt. I'm not ready to see you together."

"I don't want to make it hard on you," Vic said. "But I plan on being with her. Maybe we can work to be mindful of when you're around."

Jordan nodded, swallowed the lump in his throat. "I'd appreciate that. And I can keep working to get past it."

Vic nodded. Jordan stood and shook his hand. He stared at Vic, longing to see some part of him he recognized. But his friend was gone, leaving only a stranger who couldn't mend Jordan's empty heart.

―――――

NEARLY FIVE MONTHS AFTER JORDAN ARRIVED AT CAMP, A stranger staggered to the gate. He was haggard, dragging a broken leg. The guards brought him to Jordan at gunpoint with Moss's brother, Eric, in the lead.

"He said he knows you," Eric yelled, drawing Jordan out of the garden where he was helping. "Said you'll vouch for him."

Jordan pulled off his gloves and tossed them on the rich red soil. He wiped the sweat from his forehead as he walked toward the man. He drew close to him, staring at his face, but Jordan didn't recognize him. "Sorry. I don't know you."

"I've been working," the man rasped. "From the inside."

Jordan jerked back from the words as if he'd been slapped. He leaned forward to inspect the man's face. There was a thick beard where there wasn't one before and one of his eyes was swollen shut. But it was him. Jordan couldn't unsee him now that he knew.

"McCoy," he said. "Holy shit. You look god-awful."

Eric looked between them. "Is he good, man?"

Jordan nodded. "He's good. This is the man who helped us escape the police."

Eric gave him a hard look. He'd heard the story from his brother of the officer who betrayed his own to let them out. Jordan knew Eric had always believed the cop was working an angle.

"I'll take him to Lady Q," Jordan said, trying to stop Eric before he made things hard. The other guards had started to walk away, but Eric stood there, weighing his decision. Jordan put a hand on Eric's shoulder and said, "I trust him, E. And you trust me. You've done your part. I'll get him to Lady Q to do hers."

Eric nodded, but unstrapped the gun from its holster. "Fine, but take this. One wrong move and you shoot him."

"Look at his leg, man. He's not going anywhere."

"I'll feel better knowing you're armed," Eric said.

Jordan smiled and reached for the gun. "Okay. But only because you asked so nice."

Eric met his eyes, his face melting into the easy grin that seemed a family trait. He gave a nod and headed off after the other guards.

"Thank you," McCoy said, his voice a hoarse mess.

"Let's get you a drink," Jordan said. "After that you're going to tell me exactly what happened to you."

McCoy shook his head. "No time. They're coming."

"Who?"

"The cops. Every damn one of 'em."

"Shit," Jordan hissed. "That's what, nearly five hundred?" McCoy nodded and Jordan said, "Okay, we need to find Lady Q right now."

"Do you trust her?"

"Of course."

McCoy nodded. "There's a mole, Adler. Someone in this camp. If they see me, I'm dead."

Jordan looked around. Plenty of people had seen him already. The guards, the farmers, hell, anyone could be watching them right now. He pulled McCoy's arm over his shoulder and hoisted the weight off his damaged leg. McCoy's mouth pulled tight as he held back a scream, but the moment passed and Jordan's help seemed to lessen the pain.

They moved as fast as they could, avoiding the open areas as much as possible and sticking to side streets. By the time they reached Lady Q's place, Keelan was outside waiting for them.

"I heard he was here," she said.

Jordan nodded. "Taking him to see the boss."

"I don't know what story he told to get in," she said, "but you know you can't trust him. It'd be better for everyone if we killed him right now."

"I know you don't have a great love for the law, but McCoy has something important to tell Lady Q. She can decide whether to believe him or not."

"Jordan, come on. You know I'm right."

He pressed his lips together. "You need to move, Keelan."

"Or what?" she asked, raising her brows.

"Or I'll make you move," he said.

"You think you can?"

Jordan shook his head. "I hope I never have to find out."

They stared at one another for only a moment before Keelan stepped to the side, ushering them up the steps. In the foyer, one of Lady Q's bodyguards met them and ran a message to her chamber. Jordan expected her to appear as she did on his first day, but she didn't. Instead she had them sent to her receiving room to wait for her arrival.

She didn't keep them waiting long, a quarter of an hour perhaps, but every minute mattered when an army was at your door. She stalked into the room wearing her usual leather jumpsuit, her hair pulled back in a bun.

"I apologize for the delay," she said, leaning back on her settee. "You caught me in the bath."

Jordan said, "Sorry, but this was urgent."

"Yes, that's what you told my guard. So get to it."

"This is Officer McCoy. He works for the city's police department."

She waved her hand dismissively. "I know who he is, Jordan. My eyes are everywhere."

"Then you know about the attack," McCoy said. "Or your eyes are compromised."

She sat up. "What are you talking about?"

"The police," McCoy said. "They're on their way. They should be here in an hour."

"For fuck's sake, Jordan. Why didn't you tell me it was urgent?"

"We need to evacuate," Jordan said.

Keelan burst into the room, drawing all eyes to her. She pointed to McCoy and spat, "Don't listen to a fuckin' word he says."

Q raised one brow. "Explain."

"He's a cop. You can't trust him. Whatever lies he's telling, you can bet he has his own agenda."

"Jesus Christ, Keelan," Jordan said. "He's here to help us. They're sending their whole force at us."

"Our people can handle it. They've been training, preparing for a moment like this."

"They'll be outnumbered five to one. And that's if you could use every single person living here. Accounting for elderly, sick, and children, we've got about eighty to their five hundred," Jordan said.

"We'll have the advantage. They lost the element of surprise, thanks to McCoy."

"I thought you didn't believe him. Now you're saying he gave us an advantage."

She waved her hand dismissively and said, "And we have the wall. Not to mention they don't know the terrain."

"They'll have vehicles," McCoy said. "They can get through that wall with no problem."

Lady Q raised her hand, silencing their arguments. "We have to get them out of here. Better to live and fight another day."

She turned to leave, Jordan and Keelan following behind. Jordan asked, "What about McCoy?"

"Leave him to rest. We've got work to do and he'll just be in the way."

When they reached the steps outside, Keelan asked, "Are you really going to do this?"

"Are you questioning my decision?" Q asked, her eyes dark pools in a face of stone.

"No," she said. "Of course not. It's just that we've been preparing for this for years."

"It's too risky. We're clearing out," Quincy said.

"It's the best choice," Jordan said.

Keelan put her hands on her hips. "Lady Q, please—"

"There's nothing else to discuss," Quincy said as she stormed past her.

A gun's safety clicked off. Quincy stopped in her tracks.

"I'm sorry you feel that way," Keelan said.

Quincy slowly turned back to face Keelan. She lifted her hands, trying to keep her eyes on the girl's face instead of the gun. "Think about what you're doing, K. You know I always do what is best for the camp."

"I know you do. But I can't let you do this."

"It's you," Jordan said. "You're the mole."

Keelan winced. "I'm doing what needs to be done for the city to survive. This rebellion has to stop."

"What about Aunt Aysie? What would she—"

"She's a fool," Keelan cut in. "She can't get past her own prejudice to see what could be. Just like you."

"Keelan, we can work something out," Quincy said.

"No, we can't. I'm sorry."

A gunshot erupted.

Jordan watched red blossom on the front of Keelan's shirt. She stared down at her hand as she dipped two fingers in the blood. She looked up, wide-eyed, turning her gaze first to Quincy, then Jordan.

"You," she said, her bloody fingers pointing to Jordan, miming the way he still had his gun drawn on her. "You shot me."

"I'm sorry," he said. And he was.

She hit her knees, leaning forward, her wild ruby curls sinking toward the ground. Quincy stepped forward and knelt by her side. She helped Keelan to the ground, petting her hair and face while she whispered to her.

When Quincy stood, Jordan knew Keelan was dead. He opened his mouth to say something, but the words wouldn't come. Quincy put her hand on his shoulder and said, "I know," then passed him as she went to gather her people.

CHAPTER 9

t was cold near the river. They followed it south, moving away from the city. The people trekked in silence. Fear was palpable, a thing that journeyed with them.

Jordan walked at the back of the caravan, trying to avoid the dark glances and hateful stares. Lady Q stepped up beside him and put her hand on his shoulder. She said, "Don't let it bother you that they're angry. They don't know what happened. But they will, once we're safe. And they'll forgive you."

"I get it," Jordan said. "I murdered their friend."

"You *saved* me from a traitor. And you are their friend, too."

Jordan saw Vic marching back through the line. He stopped short when his eyes met Jordan's. Lady Q looked between them as they stood staring at each other, each unsure how to cross the chasm between them.

She nodded toward Vic and asked, "You ready?"

"Yeah," he said.

"Ready for what?" Jordan asked.

Quincy stopped walking, letting distance build between them and the rest of the group. Once out of earshot, she said, "Vic is going back to take out the city's water tower."

Jordan's brows shot up. "How?"

Vic smirked. "I've got a couple things up my sleeve."

"If you need help, I can get it for you," Q said. "Now isn't the time to let your ego come before the needs of the group."

Vic shook his head. "I can handle it."

Jordan saw Vic's pale eyes flick away when he said it. It was Vic's tell every time they played cards; Vic was lying, but there was far more on the line than a handful of crumpled dollars.

"You'll need help," Jordan said. "I'll come with you."

It was Vic's turn to look surprised. Jordan shrugged at the look and waved his hand toward the group, saying, "I can't stay with them. Not after Keelan."

"They'll come around," Quincy assured.

"Maybe. But until then, at least I can be useful. Plus I don't want Vic getting all the credit."

Vic chuckled. "That I can believe." His face was serious in an instant when he asked, "Are you sure you're up for it?"

"You don't think I can handle it?"

Vic held his hands up, waving away Jordan's words. "I know you're capable. I just don't think you'll be happy with yourself afterwards."

Jordan gritted his teeth and said, "Maybe you don't know me as well as you think."

"Maybe," Vic said. He stepped past them, heading off toward the woods. Fifteen feet away he stopped, though he didn't turn around. "You coming?"

Jordan took a step toward Vic, but Quincy caught his arm and said, "Come back to us, Jordan. Okay?"

He nodded. "I'll see you soon."

IT WAS DARK. SILENT. THEY TRUDGED THROUGH THE WOODS, stumbling over roots and holes, but neither dared turn on their flashlights; the police might not be near enough to see the light, but there could still be guards near the water tower.

Jordan's glock dug into his side with each step, a constant reminder of what was to come. He watched Vic's M21 slap against his back as they walked. Jordan remembered the day Vic's father had given it to him. He'd told Vic the story of his great-great-grandfather who had fought in the Vietnam War and how his old Springfield had been passed from father to son, one generation to the next. Vic was so proud of the gun, but more so the way his father recognized him for who he was. The next day, Mr. Spencer was gone, and Vic never saw him alive again.

"He always knew, didn't he?"

"Hm?" Vic asked, turning his head toward him.

"Your father. He understood."

Vic stopped. "Why would you ask that?"

"I've been staring at your gun for hours. Made me think about the day he gave it to you."

Vic looked off, puffing out a slow breath. "Yeah, I think he did."

"Remember how we skipped dinner that night because we were so busy cleaning it?"

Vic smiled. "We squirreled peanut butter and crackers to my room, defying Mom's 'no food out of the kitchen' rule."

"Remember how mad she was when she found us passed out with crackers all over the bed?" Jordan winced.

Vic chuckled as he shook his head. "It was a good day. One of the best."

"We've had a few."

"More than most people, I think. We've been lucky." He turned and continued through the woods, Jordan falling in line behind him.

Jordan pressed his lips together in a grim smile and muttered, "We've never been lucky."

———

JORDAN SAW THE WATER TOWER IN THE DISTANCE. VIC TOLD HIM there had once been a fence around the perimeter, but there was no longer any trace of it. Now the trees marked the perimeter of a vast expanse of cleared ground, covered in knee-high dead grass, encircling the city's poisoned water supply.

He paced back and forth between two tall trees he didn't recognize, trying to remember to remain in the shadows. Vic had been gone just over ten minutes. It wasn't enough time for Jordan to worry yet, but he was. He hadn't liked the idea of splitting up, but Vic assured him it would be quicker for him to scout for guards without the anxiety of caring for Jordan.

Jordan wanted to be annoyed with the decision, he had tried to be, but he wasn't. He was out of his element, whereas Vic was accustomed to sneaking around in this strange double life he lived.

A rustling sounded to Jordan's left. He jerked, brandishing his gun.

"Just me," Vic said, appearing like a phantom.

Jordan sighed, trying to still his hammering heart. "You scared the shit out of me."

"Sorry," Vic said, though his mouth quirked up in a smile. "But hey, you moved pretty quick. I might make something of you yet."

Jordan pursed his lips, but his smartass retort turned to dust in his mouth as he saw the way Vic looked at him. Like a friend. Like nothing was different between them. And Jordan wanted nothing more than for that to be true.

"Maybe," he said. He smiled, surprised at how strange it felt, as if he wasn't sure exactly how to do it. He shook away the thought and asked, "So what did you find?"

"Turns out the march on our camp included most of the

guys who were guarding this place. I only saw six of them around the tower."

"Six? Against two. Not great odds."

"I know. Almost makes you feel bad for them."

When Jordan didn't respond, Vic's smile faded and he said, "Hey man, if you can't do this, now's the time to say so."

Jordan whispered, "I'm scared, Vic."

Vic closed the gap between them and wrapped his arms around his friend. "I know. Me, too. But this is our chance, J. Maybe our only chance, to end this."

Jordan froze at Vic's touch. He stood rigid for several seconds before the hardness between them finally melted and Jordan returned the embrace. After a moment he asked, "Do you really think this will fix things?"

Vic pulled back to look in Jordan's eyes. "No."

"Then why do it?"

"Because maybe I'm wrong. Maybe this is what it takes to start a revolution."

"Or it gets us killed."

Vic nodded. "Maybe."

"You're okay with that, with dying? What about Reeva?"

Vic flinched and took a step back. "She knows what's at stake."

Jordan shook his head and took a deep breath. "You're not leaving her, you sonuvabitch. We're gonna do our job here and you're going home to her. Understand me?"

Vic nodded.

"Good. Now tell me what to do."

––––––

THE FIRST FOUR GUARDS WERE EASY TO KILL. EACH WAS ALONE, patrolling the tree line. Jordan distracted them while Vic slipped behind them. He was surprised by the first one; he'd never imagined Vic would have the fortitude to stab someone in the kidney before slicing through their vocal cords. Jordan puked behind a tree. The second was a little easier to watch, the third more so. By the fourth, he wasn't even queasy.

They donned the hats and jackets of the guards. Jordan swiped a gun off the last one, though he wasn't entirely sure he knew how to use it. Vic had made them split up again. He thought it would look suspicious if they headed to the tower together. Jordan was supposed to wait until he heard the first gunshot, so he'd look like he was responding to the danger. After watching the way Vic dispatched with the other guards, he wasn't worried anymore.

He shifted his weight foot-to-foot, his eyes flitting through the dark. He looked down at his stolen uniform. There was blood spattered across the nametag on the right side. *Robertson.* Jordan wiped his sleeve across the white nametag; tiny pink stains remained as the only evidence of this man's life.

A gunshot cracked through the silent night.

Jordan bolted for the tower. His breath came faster, blood pounding through his ears, as the lights of the tower grew larger. He almost didn't hear the second shot. Vic must've run into the other guard.

A third shot.

And a fourth.

Shit. Shit. Shit. The word echoed through Jordan's head as he raced for the tower. Something was wrong. There were supposed to be two guards. Two. As good as Vic was, he shouldn't need four shots.

He skidded to a stop when he saw two guards standing over three bodies. He was too loud, too *Jordan,* and the guards spun on him, guns raised.

"Whoa, hey," Jordan said, throwing his hands in the air. "It's just me."

"Me who?" one asked, stepping toward him.

"Robertson," Jordan said, trying his damnedest to sound confident.

The guy in the front lowered his gun, but the second guy hesitated. Jordan took a deep breath, trying to figure out how to bluff his way through. "I heard shots," he said. "What's goin' on?"

"Eddie caught this guy snoopin' around the tower," the front guy said, hooking his finger over his shoulder toward Eddie. "He done shot Mara."

"Damn. You got him though, right?" Jordan asked. "He's dead?"

Eddie's gun came up quick. He growled, "The real Robertson would know we take prisoners alive."

Jordan scoffed. "Of course I know that. But with Mara shot—"

Eddie's gun dipped and a shot rang out. Jordan yelped as the bullet seared the flesh of his left leg. He stumbled, hitting the ground on all fours.

He could hear the guards approaching, but as he retreated into his head their voices sounded as if they were a long way off. His mind raced through the scenario looking for a gap to expose. He was hurt, but he was pretty sure the bullet only grazed him. They were coming toward him, but right now he was free to move. They might shoot him again if he tried, but perhaps Eddie wasn't a good shot.

Jordan sprang from the ground, pain shooting through his leg. He crossed the distance between them and tackled one of the men to the ground. They rolled, each trying to gain the advantage.

"Hold still so I can shoot him!" the other guard yelled.

The man wrestling Jordan reached down and jabbed a finger into Jordan's leg where the bullet had grazed him. Jordan jerked the limb, trying to maneuver it away, but the guard pinned his down and pressed his fist against the wound, leaning down with all his weight. Jordan screamed, bucked, tried to throw the man off, but he held firm. The pain was intense, drawing away his very will to fight, and Jordan saw the edges of his vision go black.

As his eyes closed, he heard a gunshot echo through the dark.

CHAPTER 10

Jordan opened his eyes to see Vic's bright smile hovering over him.

"Helluva distraction," Vic said.

"Wha-what?" Jordan asked. He pushed himself up, wincing at the pain in his leg.

"I wasn't sure what you were doing at first. Fucking brilliant."

Jordan shrugged. "Thanks?"

"No, thank you. We'd be dead if not for your quick thinking." He reached his hand down and helped Jordan stand. "Now we need to place these charges and we can get back to the others."

Vic pulled off his boot and tipped it over. A small black bundle the size of Jordan's thumb tumbled out. Vic picked it up and handed it to Jordan, then turned up his other boot to reveal a second bundle.

"What are these?" Jordan asked.

"High density explosives," Vic said.

"Like the ones used in WWIII?"

Vic nodded. "Antoine built them. He was a munitions expert in the war. Says his bombs were used in the battle for D.C."

"Shit," Jordan said, turning the small box over in his hands.

Vic chuckled. "Yeah. They'll be fine for what we want. Probably won't even need them both. You okay to walk?"

Jordan nodded, testing his leg. It hurt, bad, but he could walk. He limped behind Vic toward the water tower, listening to his instructions.

"While I'm up top, I want you to look for a weak spot on the legs. The detonator has a decent range, so we'll blow it once we get back to the woods."

Jordan nodded. He glanced up at Vic as he started climbing, noticing the dark stain on his side. "You're bleeding."

"Just a scratch," Vic said. He winced as he climbed another wrung.

"That's a lot of blood for a scratch." Jordan shook his head. "Let's put them both on legs and get out of here while we still can."

"It's no good unless we can be sure the tower is unusable."

"Will it really make a difference?" Jordan mumbled.

"It has to," Vic replied. "It's all we've got."

Vic was nearing the top when Jordan heard the shouts from the woods. He turned to see a squadron of soldiers running through the grass toward the tower.

He looked up. Vic's hand was reaching for the side of the tank when the litany of shots erupted. Jordan watched Vic's body jerk as the bullets hit him. He fell backwards, as if in slow motion. He didn't tumble, as Jordan thought he might. No, it was as if he were plopping on the bed after a long day.

And then he hit the ground.

Jordan expected the crunch, like when Gene had fallen. But it didn't come. Just silence. Loud, deafening silence. It was as if the whole world had stopped, pausing in a moment of silence for his friend.

Jordan felt a sting in his belly. A bug bite, surely. He

looked down, surprised to see blood on his hand as he touched the itch.

It was so quiet.

Jordan couldn't stand any longer. His knees buckled underneath him. He crawled, inch by inch, making his way to Vic. He fell on top of him. Jordan looked down at Vic's face. His eyes were beautiful—pale blue, like his grandma had said the sky used to be—but they were dull now, lifeless.

He traced his finger along Vic's forehead, brushing the dark hair from his eyes as he'd seen Vic do a hundred million times. He put his hand on Vic's cheek, then gently pressed his lips against Vic's.

"Goodbye, my friend. I love you."

Jordan rummaged in Vic's pocket, withdrawing the detonator. He lay back on the ground beside Vic and stared up. He smiled. There, far above, the perma-clouds were parted ever so slightly. He could see a single star shining like the promise of tomorrow.

He pushed the detonator and closed his eyes.

ABOUT THE AUTHOR

Shelly Jarvis began working on speculative fictions thanks to a writing assignment in Mrs. Bettijane Burger's eleventh grade English class, but her passion for writing developed at seven when she wrote a Halloween tale about a witch and a ghost who became best friends.

An avid science fiction and fantasy reader, Shelly spends a large portion of each new day dwelling in other worlds.

Shelly enjoys spending time with her wacky spouse, her wonderful nephews, and her rescue pups, Gimli, Butters, Fergus, and Pickles. She currently resides near Charleston, West Virginia, in the wild and wonderful mountains that have her heart.

Learn more at www.ShellyJarvis.com

ALSO BY SHELLY JARVIS

City of Trials

Lady Mad Max **meets LGBTQ+** *Hunger Games!*

With Nova's inevitable outcast from the Raiders drawing near, she'll do anything to earn a permanent place among her nomadic found family. When she sees a stranger alone in the grasslands, she knows this is her chance to capture an outsider and offer him as a tribute in an attempt to gain acceptance.

But when they refuse her gift, Nova has to leave the safety of the Raiders and return the stranger to the gods' domain by crossing the ruined earth in a final bid to gain her family's favor and save herself from banishment. Fortunately, she won't have to travel alone. In addition to the captured stranger who is cursed by the gods, she leads a motley band of Raiders who have volunteered to accompany her in an effort to remove the stranger's threat from their people.

Together they make their way to the City of Trials, where the world of humans and the home of the gods collide. Along the way, Nova finds her heart warring between two sides of who she could be: half is with Thoa the Bonecutter, the brooding warrior who seeks to protect her, the Raiders, and all she's known since they rescued her as a child. The other half embraces this stranger, Krew of the starfolk, his desire to see her free, and a chance for a strange new life she can hardly imagine. Putting herself on the line for them both, she finds herself in a deathmatch, facing things the only way she knows how: dealing death to all who endanger the fragile life she's creating for herself.

In a city built on the blood of the strong, only the fiercest survive, especially when the gods turn out to be something far from what she'd envisioned and vastly more dangerous—other humans.

———

The Dreamwalker

Even among the Chosen, there is one who is *more*.

When 16 year old Kate Watzen sees her future in a dream, she can hardly believe the life of a Chosen could really be hers. Unlike the other teenagers on her home planet, she's had no training to draw out the legendary Gifts the galaxy's peacekeepers are known for. Despite her concerns, she goes to be tested anyway, only to discover she is exactly who the Chosen have been waiting for.

Moving from her small farming community to study at a school full of hundreds of aliens, Kate's Gifts begin to manifest, drawing her into the focus of a ruthless man, Lord Ruark, who wishes to use her abilities to gain access to an object of great knowledge and power, the Book of the Golden One.

Kate's unwillingness to help him leads to a confrontation endangering all those she loves, including her best friend, Ben, who will do anything to protect her, and the stranger who's been training her through dreams, James, whose mysterious past may lead her into more danger than she realizes.

Through these trials, Kate discovers the strength that has been dormant within her, showing her that she is anything but ordinary, and the small town life she had was full of mystery, adventure, intrigue, and a betrayal far beyond anything she could have imagined.

The Fall of Water House

The Elementalists are coming, and with them, Rosalinde's future.

Every year the kingdom of Talabrih has a massive celebration to honor the elements. There's swordplay and jousting, feasts and dancing, and the biggest draw of all--The Great Match. The highest ranking noble of twenty years of age will be given the chance to select their match from all the other nobles of the same age. This year, the highest ranking noble is Princess Rosalinde.

She's known that she would be forced into this since she was a child.

In former years, she even relished the thought of choosing a daring Elementalist who had proven his love for her. But as the celebration approaches and she prepares herself for the competition that will decide her future, the thought of choosing one of these men without the potential for true love seems like fate's cruelest trick.

Little does she know, fate can play dirtier still.

When her father goes missing during the events of the Great Match, Ros quickly realizes she's the only one who can find him. Armed with her violent Tsunami magic and the assistance of competitors from all the houses--Air, Earth, Fire, Water, and Night--she must track the King across the country and bring him back before all hell breaks loose and their kingdom ends up in a war for the throne...all while figuring out which of the Elementalists is worthy to be the future king, and hopefully, the love of her life.

Black Sea Bright Song

Evan is in a real life version of kiss/marry/kill and things are getting tense. With newly discovered sea witch powers and Sirens on the loose, how's a girl supposed to navigate first love?

Mermaid Princess Evannia is in lust. She's caught up in a secret affair with Rafe, her raven-eyed guard, despite knowing she won't be allowed to choose him on her Thrice Day. *Ugh, Thrice Day*. She'll turn 20, the age that Mer are *finally* considered adults. But she'll also be officially named heir of the Triton kingdom AND have a gigantic celebration where she'll have to choose her future husband. That is, if she even makes it to her Thrice Day without her mother forcing her into an alliance with Prince Calix, the future king of neighboring kingdom of Protea.

But none of that matters when the Sirens attack. Triton's oldest enemy has returned, their silver eyes flashing and seductive songs pulling at Evan's soul. She doesn't know what they want, only that their tridents are aimed at her. Forced to flee the ocean to avoid capture, Princess Evannia finds herself in the last place she ever imagined.

The sea isn't safe, but land is full of the unknown, and worse, humans. Outside the protected life she's lived, surrounded by human inventions and wonder, she finds her spirit--wild, unafraid, fierce. The woman who returns to the sea to save her kingdom is not the same naïve princess who fled: she is the blood of Poseidon and she will not run.

www.ingramcontent.com/pod-product-compliance
Lightning Source LLC
Chambersburg PA
CBHW031728170626
46808CB00005B/1935